The
Orphan Game

OTHER LOTHROP BOOKS BY BARBARA COHEN

The Carp in the Bathtub
Thank You, Jackie Robinson
I Am Joseph
Yussel's Prayer
Gooseberries to Oranges
King of the Seventh Grade
Molly's Pilgrim
Here Come the Purim Players!
Roses
Coasting
Even Higher
The Christmas Revolution
The Donkey's Story
Canterbury Tales

The
Orphan Game

by Barbara Cohen

illustrated by Diane deGroat

Lothrop, Lee & Shepard Books · New York

First Edition 1 2 3 4 5 6 7 8 9 10

Library of Congress Cataloging in Publication Data
Cohen, Barbara. The orphan game.
Summary: Vacationing at Long Beach Island, four cousins engage in a variety of
activities, including pretending to be orphans, raising money for a trip to Atlantic
City, and avoiding a whiny cousin named Miranda. [1. Cousins—Fiction.
2. Beaches—Fiction] I. DeGroat, Diane, ill. II. Title.
PZ7.C6595Or 1988 [Fic] 87-29340
ISBN 0-688-07615-7

*Remembering Felice
"Wishing all year
could be summer"*

One

Sally opened up Aunt Nan's striped canvas sand chair and settled it just a yard from the water's edge. The tide was going out; her beach bag and her Jersey Tomato beach towel were safe. She sat down carefully, and sighed. She was comfortable—very, very comfortable.

She opened the bag and pulled out her notebook and a pencil. Putting the eraser end in her mouth, she thought about a new poem. Alone on the beach—that was the best situation for making up poems. She decided to write one about Jenny.

> Jenny has eyes like two black
>   rocks.

That didn't sound so nice. She crossed it out and tried again.

> Jenny has eyes like two dark
>   stars. . . .
> And so does that clown Octavia.

That was good. An ordinary person reading the poem would think that Octavia was someone else. But a member of the Four Seasons club—Sally Berg, her twin sister Emily, and her cousins Jenny and Jake Alexander—would know that Jenny and Octavia were actually the same person.

"Sally!"

She pretended not to hear the voice. She knew who it was. It was Emily. If ignored long enough, maybe she'd go away. Not that Sally disliked Emily. After all, though they bore almost no resemblance to each other in looks or personality, they *were* twins. But at the moment, Sally liked the poem she was writing better.

Emily plopped down on the Jersey Tomato towel, put her hand on Sally's shoulder, and shook her so hard Sally felt as if her hair were going to fall out of her scalp. "Cut it out," she exclaimed.

"I can't help it." Emily withdrew her hand. "That's the only way to get your attention when you've got your nose in your notebook."

"I don't bother you when you want to be by yourself," Sally protested.

"I never want to be by myself," Emily returned matter-of-factly. "But it isn't just me. The others'll be here in a minute. They've got something to tell us."

Sally looked beyond Emily and saw Jenny and Jake on the path that led from their house over the dunes to the beach. They were running. It must be a matter of life and death. Sally snapped the notebook shut, folded her hands on her lap, and waited.

"They called," Emily said. "They wanted to know where you were. I said you were on the beach, and they said we had to have an emergency meeting of the Four Seasons."

"Aunt Nan went shopping," Sally said.

"I know that. We don't need Aunt Nan every time we have a Four Seasons meeting."

"Without Aunt Nan there wouldn't be any Four Seasons," Sally reminded her. Two summers before, on a day when the Little Kids were moping around because the Big Kids had gone off without them on a bike trip to the lighthouse, Aunt Nan had suggested that they organize a private society, of which Sally, Emily, Jenny, and Jake were to be the only members. The Four Seasons, unlike most kid clubs, had survived, thanks to monthly gourmet meals at Aunt Nan's house. Even that would not have been a sufficient program to keep the organization alive if they hadn't gotten into the production of plays composed by all of them, directed by Aunt Nan, and presented at family celebrations.

And then, of course, there was the Orphan Game. Even Aunt Nan didn't know

4

about that. The Four Seasons was private; the Orphan Game was secret.

Jake threw himself down in the sand next to Sally's chair. Emily patted the towel on which she was sitting, and Jenny lowered her slim, brown, bikini-clad body to the spot indicated. She wasted no time on preliminaries. "The Big Kids are going to Atlantic City," she announced. "On the Black Whale. Tomorrow."

"Who's taking them?" Emily wondered. "Whoever it is, they'll have to take us next time."

"No one's taking them. They're going by themselves."

"What!" Sally exclaimed. "I can't believe that. I can't believe they'd be allowed to go to Atlantic City all by themselves, no matter how big they are. After all, they're not *that* big." The twins had just turned ten, and their sister Lisa was not yet thirteen. Jenny was eleven; her brother Jake was eight and a half, her sister Amy twelve, and her brother Chip almost fourteen.

"Well," Jenny explained, "they're just going on the boat by themselves. Phyllis

Slotnick and her mom and dad are going to meet them at the dock in Atlantic City. They're taking them to dinner and to a show in a hotel, for Phyllis's birthday."

Emily's wide clear eyes opened even wider. "Are they going to gamble?"

"They're too young to gamble," Jenny said. "They don't let you in the casinos unless you're twenty-one."

Jake dribbled sand over his outstretched legs. "I'd like to go to Atlantic City anyway," he said. "I'd like to see the boardwalk."

"I'd like to see a show," Sally added dreamily.

"I think all the shows in Atlantic City are dirty," Emily said.

"They can't be," Jenny pointed out. "Even the Slotnicks wouldn't take Phyllis and Amy and Chip and Lisa to see a dirty show."

"*Carnival* is at the Bellevue, starring Serena Sue Miletta. She's not much older than Lisa, and she's already been singing in movies and TV shows for seven years." There was more than a touch of envy in

Sally's voice. "In this show she plays an orphan named Lili. She falls in love with a magician, only he couldn't care less. . . ."

"OK," Emily interrupted. "We get the idea."

Jenny shook her head. "Boy, Sally, how do you know these things?"

"She reads the newspapers," Emily said. "She reads everything, even toilet paper wrappers."

"Oh, shut up," Sally grumbled.

"So what?" Jake said. "I read the toilet paper wrappers too. I also read the tomato soup cans. They're more interesting. Tomato soup cans have recipes on them."

"Forget tomato soup cans, Jake, will you?" Jenny urged. "Put your mind to something useful, like getting us to Atlantic City."

"And not by car," Sally added. "On the Black Whale. They have an accordion player on the Black Whale."

"If that play's about an orphan, we certainly should see it," Emily remarked.

"You're right, Juliette," Jake said. He was using Emily's secret name, a signal that he'd slipped into the Orphan Game. "If we could get to Atlantic City, maybe we could shake the Matron for good. She can't cross water."

Sally thumbed through the back pages of her notebook. "Listen, Marchmain, it doesn't say anything about that in the Records."

"I just decided, Julia," Jake informed them. "Write it down."

Jenny stood up. "If we're going to stay here and play the Orphan Game, I have to go back to the house and get my own towel." Then, suddenly, she sat down again. "Uh-oh, look who's coming."

The others turned, glanced in the direction Jenny faced, and quickly directed their eyes back to each other. Jake groaned and tried to bury his legs in earnest now, grabbing piles of sand and dumping them on himself in ever more rapid succession. No one said a word. In a moment, Cousin Lenny was upon them. Behind him trailed his daughter, Miranda, lugging a beach bag stuffed so full that its red-and-white-striped sides were as rigid as if they were made out of steel. "Geez," Jenny whispered. "It looks like she's planning to stay for a year."

"Hi, Lenny," Sally greeted them. "Hullo, Miranda."

"Cousin Rhoda and I are spending the day on the Cucurellos' boat," Lenny said. "Miranda is spending the day with you."

Silence greeted his announcement.

"I phoned your mother," Lenny added. "She said it's OK."

"Which mother?" Jenny snapped.

"Yours," Lenny replied. "I'm sure it's OK with the twins' mom too. We'll be back after dinner. Don't buy anything from the ice cream man. Then we can all go to the Frosted Mug for something really good."

Sally sighed. A whole day with Miranda. Ice cream wasn't sufficient payment. Anyway, last time Miranda spent the day, they'd bought cones from the ice cream man after dinner, but when Lenny and Rhoda got back, Miranda had lied. *"I didn't buy any ice cream,"* she'd said.

"OK," Lenny had replied. "Then I'll take *you* to the Frosted Mug on the way home."

Now Cousin Lenny's eyes focused on ch one of them in turn. Their faces fell away from his glance. He took off the green terry-cloth tennis hat he was wearing and dropped it on Miranda's head.

"Oh, Daddy," she whined, "I don't need a hat."

"You do need a hat, darling," he replied. "You have to wear a hat in the sun."

"I don't burn; I tan."

"The sun here isn't like the sun at home. You're not used to this glare. It could make you sick." He kissed her on the cheek. "See you later, Alligator."

"In a while, Crocodile," she replied dutifully. She didn't watch him go. She withdrew a large beach towel from her bag and arranged it so carefully that its edges were perfectly flat and straight, and not a single wrinkle marred its surface. Then without disturbing so much as a grain of sand, she sat down daintily right in the middle of it. She did not remove the hat.

Emily stood up. "Jake, you want to go in the water?"

"Sure." He leaped to his feet, dripping

mounds of sand from his legs onto Miranda's towel.

"Hey, watch out," she cried. "You're getting me all sandy."

"If you don't like the sand," he retorted, "stay off the beach."

Jenny rose to her feet too. "I'm going back up to get my towel," she said. "I'll meet you in the water."

"You want to go swimming?" Sally asked Miranda.

"No," Miranda replied. She brushed away the sand Jake had dribbled on her towel and then reached inside her bag for her needlepoint.

Each stitch of Miranda's elaborate flower design looked exactly like every other stitch. It was even neater than Jenny's rabbits. Sally wondered if Miranda was planning to hang it up wrong side out. "Why don't you want to come in?" she asked.

"Jake'll dunk me. I don't feel like being dunked."

Sally shrugged and then flew away from Miranda like a bird let out of a cage. "I'm coming, I'm coming," she screamed, even though Jake and Emily, bobbing like buoys out beyond the breakers, couldn't hear her. She plunged into the surf, breasting the waves, moving her legs and arms against the force of the water, feeling the marvelous exhilaration that coursed through her body whenever she fought against the sea. Soon she was out with Emily and Jake, to be joined moments later by Jenny.

"Come on," Jenny said. "Let's swim out farther."

Jenny's strong, even strokes carried her out as far as she dared to go without risking the lifeguard's whistle. It took the others a little while to catch up to her, but soon they were floating side by side, staring up at the sky. The four of them, together, in the middle of a cool green sea on a glaring gold and blue summer's day. That was what Sally dreamt of all winter long.

"Hey, Julia," Jenny said, "what are we doing here? How did we get here?"

"Don't you remember, Octavia? Matron can't cross water." They all agreed that Matron looked exactly like Mrs. Kresge, the cafeteria aide at Watch Mountain School, who wouldn't even allow you to mush up your Jell-O, let alone blow a straw wrapper. Like Mrs. Kresge, Matron seemed to have eyes in back of her head.

"This time," Emily said, "she won't be able to come after us. This time we'll escape from the orphanage for good."

"Maybe she can't follow us," Jake said, "but someone else can."

"Like who, Marchmain?" Emily asked.

"The Denver Horror," Jake replied. "One glance from his beady eyes, and you're turned to stone. Matron just hired him as her assistant. He came with his daughter, Miss Priss. Matron just loves her. All the grown-ups do."

"Our real mother will hate her," Emily said. "If she isn't dead. And if we ever find her."

"We'll find her, Juliette," Jenny assured her. "Don't give up hope. Start swimming. Swim hard."

Jenny lowered her feet and lifted up her head. "Hey, big one coming," she exclaimed. For the moment, the Orphan Game was suspended. Together, she and Sally mounted the wave's crest and rode it to the shore, their bodies stretched taut, their heads down, their arms reaching straight and stiff in front of them. Emily and Jake were right behind them.

They rode the next one, and the next one, and the one after that. But they couldn't stay in the water forever. Eventually, their bodies chilled, their stomachs growling with hunger, the four of them stood in a clump at the water's edge, little wavelets lapping at their ankles, the sun warming their wrinkled flesh. "Listen," Emily said, "Aunt Nan'll take us to Atlantic City. I'm sure she will. We just have to ask her."

"Who'll pay?" Jenny wondered. "Atlantic City's expensive, and she can't afford to treat the four of us when it isn't even a special occasion. Our parents would never spring for something like that."

"Ours neither," Emily added.

"Yeah," Sally grumbled. "Dad's always showing Mom some newspaper article about how the Mafia controls laundry or garbage or something else in Atlantic City. He says any state stupid enough to legalize gambling deserves what it gets. They'd sooner send us to Siberia."

"We could earn the money," Emily suggested.

"How?" Jake returned. "We're at the beach."

"What does that have to do with it? We'll think of something."

Jenny started running. The others followed her across the sand to the area, now several feet from the edge of the sea, which they had staked out as their own. Miranda still sat on her towel, her needle darting in and out of her canvas like a sunbeam. But Sally noticed that her hair was damp. Sometime while they'd been in the water she'd gone in too. But she'd kept well out of their way. They hadn't even seen her.

"Want some lunch?" Sally asked.

Carefully Miranda folded her needlepoint and placed it inside the canvas bag. She stood up, picked up the bag, and hung it on her arm. "You can leave your bag," Emily said. "We'll come right back here after we eat."

"Someone might take it," Miranda said.

"For heaven's sake, Miranda, who would want your stupid needlepoint?" Jake asked.

"It's not a stupid needlepoint. It's a really hard one, and it looks really good. It looks a lot better than Sally's."

"Which is not saying much," Sally remarked. "And I think you're a first-class crumb to mention it."

"It's not just yours," Miranda returned. "Mine is better than Emily's too. It's even better than Jenny's."

Jenny merely raised her eyebrows, but Jake snatched the bag from Miranda's arm before she realized what was happening. He ran up the beach, swinging it around above his head. "Come and get it," he called. "Come and get it if you can."

Arms and legs churning, Miranda tore after him. "Give it back to me," she screamed. But though she was two years older than he and much taller, she hadn't a chance in a thousand of catching him. He ran like the wind, even through the sand, and disappeared behind the dunes.

When Sally, Emily, and Jenny reached the twins' house, they found Miranda crying on the deck and no sign of Jake. "He's going to throw it into the ocean," she sobbed. "I know he is."

"No, he won't," Jenny assured her.

She sniffled and wiped her nose with the back of her hand. "Where is he, then?"

"Probably at our house."

"No, he's not at your house," Miranda said. "I didn't see him go by."

"He ducked over the dunes."

Except for a narrow path leading to the street, the dunes were protected by snow fences from the erosion caused by the endless parade of bathers on their way to the beach. "He could get a ticket for that!" Miranda exclaimed. She sounded as if it were a crime second only to murder.

"He did it anyway," Sally returned drily. She didn't bother to tell Miranda that very early their first morning in Beach Haven, she and Emily had helped Jake and Jenny remove some slats from the fencing so that Julia, Juliette, Octavia, and Marchmain could hide from Matron behind the mounds of sand.

"I'll go get your precious bag." Jenny

ambled across the deck and disappeared down the steps.

Emily entered the house. For a moment, Sally regarded Miranda's red nose and puffy eyes. "Come on, stop sniffling," she said. "Let's go in. Let's see what there is for lunch."

Miranda indulged in a final snort as she followed Sally into the big front room with its huge picture window looking out to the beach. A combination living room, dining room, and kitchen, the room ran the whole width of the house. Emily was peering into the refrigerator. Aunt Nan was sitting at the kitchen counter eating an enormously fat chicken sandwich. "You want one of these?" she asked Emily.

"No, thanks," Emily said. "I'll have peanut butter and jelly." She carried two jars from the fridge to the counter.

"How can you prefer peanut butter and jelly to my delicious chicken?" Aunt Nan wondered.

"I'd like a sandwich made out of your delicious chicken, Aunt Nan," said Miranda.

"Would you? At least you've got some taste." Aunt Nan looked up at Miranda as she reached for the foil pan in which the remains of last night's dinner rested in congealed gravy. "Miranda! You've been crying."

Sympathy set Miranda off again. Aunt Nan rushed over, knelt beside her, put her arms around her, and hugged her close. "What's the matter, Miranda? What's the matter, honey girl?"

In spite of her tears, Miranda managed quite a definite reply. "Jake threw my needlepoint in the ocean."

Aunt Nan's mouth dropped open in horror. "He didn't," Emily exclaimed. "She's making a fuss over something that didn't even happen."

"Well, he grabbed my bag, didn't he? He ran away with it, didn't he?" Miranda dabbed at her eye with her knuckle. "If he didn't throw it in the ocean, what did he do with it?"

"Here it is, crybaby." Jake appeared, followed by Jenny. The screen door slammed behind them. Once again, Jake swung the bag around his head, but this time he let it drop at Miranda's feet. She picked it up and clutched it to her chest as if it were her child.

Aunt Nan faced Jake, fury in her face. "Why do you tease Miranda? She's never done anything to you. Besides, she's your cousin."

"Not my *first* cousin," Jake retorted. He took a huge, ripe peach from the bowl on the counter and bit into it. A blessing, Sally thought. For a while, he'd be too busy battling sticky peach juice to cause trouble.

"It's not only Jake," Miranda sobbed. "It's all of them. They all tease me."

Cousin Lenny, Cousin Rhoda, and Miranda had spent a month at the beach once before, when Miranda was really little, like six. Had she been a whiner and tattletale then? Sally couldn't remember. Miranda and her family lived in Denver. Colorado was full of beautiful mountains. Why had they bothered to come all the way to New Jersey for vacation?

But of course Sally knew why. It wasn't just for the ocean. It was so that Rhoda could be with *her* cousins, Mom and Aunt

Lou, the way the Four Seasons were to-gether. But so far as the Four Seasons were concerned, it had been a mess from the moment Miranda had arrived, a week be-fore. The Bergs and Alexanders had helped Lenny and Rhoda move into their cottage. Miranda hadn't carried in a single bag or box. "I have a stomachache," she'd whined, throwing herself down on her unmade bed. "From the trip."

"Convenient cramps," Cousin Rhoda had commented drily.

"Leave her alone," Cousin Lenny said. "You know she gets carsick."

"She grew out of that five years ago," Rhoda replied. But she didn't push it, and Miranda had remained on the bed, her eyes closed and her lips drawn down, an island of martyred stillness amidst a swirl of ac-tivity.

Since then, the Four Seasons had been forced to put up with Miranda for at least part of each day. And now, today, for the second time, they were stuck with her for most of their waking hours.

Sally pulled a tissue from the box on the

counter and dropped it in Miranda's lap. Miranda picked it up blew her nose, and then headed for the door. "Where're you going, darling?" Aunt Nan asked.

"I'll sit on the deck," Miranda replied. "I'll sit on the deck and do my needle-point."

"But what about your lunch?"

"I'm not hungry right now."

"I'll fix a sandwich and bring it out to you," Aunt Nan called after her. She shoved a croissant in the microwave to warm. "You kids are bad," she said, "really bad. I'm ashamed of you."

"Miranda's a pain," Jenny muttered. "We don't have to like her just because she's re-lated to us."

"She's a lovely girl," Aunt Nan insisted. "So pretty, and so talented."

Jake snorted. "She lies," Jenny said.

"She does not," Nan retorted. "I've never heard her tell a lie."

"I have." Sally knew Jenny was remem-bering the ice cream.

"Like what?" Aunt Nan asked.

But of course Jenny wouldn't say. Jenny wasn't a tattletale.

"She whines too," Emily added.

"Look who's talking," Jake commented.

"She's nearly eleven, and she still whines," Emily retorted. "I grew out of it."

"What did you grow out of?" Led by Chip, the Big Kids stomped into the house, slamming the screen door behind them.

"Whining," Emily explained.

Lisa wrinkled her nose. "You wouldn't know it by me."

Sally rushed to Emily's defense. "She whines less than she used to. Much less."

"I wish I had a twin who always stuck up for me." Lisa tugged at one of Sally's pigtails.

Sally pulled away. "What's true is true," she insisted.

Chip reached toward the pan of cold chicken. Aunt Nan tapped his hand lightly with a spatula. "Wait 'til I'm done making Miranda's sandwich."

"Why does Miranda get first choice?" Chip complained.

"Because the kids were mean to her. They could offer me bags of emeralds and rubies, and I wouldn't let them eat one bite of my chicken now."

Lisa stared at her. "Boy, Nanny, you're in a bad mood today."

"I was in a good mood before the Little Kids were nasty to Miranda." She arranged the completed sandwich, a bottle of soda, a napkin, a peach, and some cookies on a tray as carefully as if she were going to paint them, and carried it out to the deck.

"You'd think I beat Miranda up or something," Jake complained. "She can't take the littlest joke."

The Big Kids gathered around the counter and began picking at the pan of chicken. "Do I really want to go to Atlantic City tomorrow with a bunch of girls?" Chip wondered.

"Well, I'd go with a bunch of boys," Amy said. "It'd be worth it."

"It's not fair," Emily complained. "It's just not fair."

"What's unfair about it?" Lisa returned

airily. "You don't go everywhere we go, you don't do everything we do. You're much younger than we are."

"What'll we wear?" Amy wondered.

"C'mon, let's see what I've got, and then we'll go to your house and see what you've got."

"I didn't bring anything really nice with me," Amy said regretfully. "I mean, who thought we'd need fancy clothes at the beach?"

"We'll throw something together," Lisa assured her. They hurried down the hall to the bedroom that Lisa shared with Aunt Nan. Chip drifted out of the house as Aunt Nan reentered the room, carrying Miranda's now-empty tray.

"Listen, Nanny," Emily said, "we need to have a Four Seasons meeting."

"Do you?" Aunt Nan replied coldly. "Then go ahead, have one."

"But we need you, Aunt Nan," Jake said, taking her hand. "We can't do without you."

"Don't think you can con me, Jake Alexander." But Aunt Nan let her hand remain in his. She'd never been able to resist Jake.

"I call this meeting of the Four Seasons to order," Jenny announced quickly as Jake half escorted, half pulled Aunt Nan to a chair. "The topic of this meeting is getting to Atlantic City."

"On the Black Whale," Emily chimed in.

"And seeing a show," Sally added.

"Will you take us, Aunt Nan?" Jake asked, gazing at her with soulful eyes.

"You don't have to pay for it," Sally interjected.

"I don't think I could," Aunt Nan said. "I'm just a working girl."

"We'll find a way to raise the money," Emily said. "But we need you to help with that, and then to go with us—because, you know, they'd never let us go alone."

"Maybe your parents should go with you."

"No, *no,* NO," Jake cried. "It has to be you."

"Yes," Emily agreed. "You're much more fun than the grown-ups."

"Thank you," Aunt Nan returned with

a grin, obviously understanding Emily's remark to be a compliment. Their grand-mother's younger sister, she was some-where—no one knew exactly where—between fifty and sixty years old.

"Then it's OK?" Jenny asked. "You'll help us?"

"Yes," Aunt Nan replied. "I'll help. On one condition."

"Anything," Jake said. "Anything you say."

"You mean that?" Her eyes locked with his.

"Oh, yes," they all exclaimed, more or less in unison.

"OK," Aunt Nan said softly. "Stop teasing Miranda."

"We will," Jenny said. "We promise."

Sally crossed her fingers behind her back as she, Emily, Jenny, and Jake nodded sol-emn agreement. But they weren't lying, not really. They'd just keep out of Miranda's way, that's all. They couldn't tease her if they weren't with her.

Two

Before-dinner cocktails were at the twins' house. The table on the deck was laden with cheese, crackers, sliced vegetables, pates, dips, and bottles of all shapes and sizes. The grown-ups—even Aunt Nan—reclined on chaise lounges, talking and drinking from clear plastic glasses. The Big Kids were in Atlantic City. Emily, Jenny, and Jake sat in a circle on the floor playing hearts, crunching corn chips, and sipping soda from disposable cans.

Sally disliked card games, perhaps because she was so bad at them. She perched on the rail and gazed at the beach. Far out, surfers floated, waiting for the perfect wave, and beyond them, along the horizon, she could see a few fishing boats unwilling to give up until the last drop of daylight had drained from the sky. A couple stood at the water's edge, wrapped in a single towel. Otherwise, the beach was empty.

She turned and glanced at her parents. Her mother was walking around refilling empty glasses. Her father and Uncle Andrew were engaged in a passionate argument about the president, whom Dad hated and Uncle Andrew admired excessively. Lenny, Rhoda, and Miranda hadn't even arrived yet. It would be a long time until dinner.

She wandered over to the card game. "You guys want to play on the beach?" she asked.

"When we're done with this game," Jenny said.

"It could be dark by then."

Emily picked a card from Jake's hand. Jake grinned. "You rat!" Emily screamed.

"Emily, you're a jerk," Jenny told her. "Now I know you've got the queen of spades."

They were absorbed in their game. Sally didn't mind. It would be pleasant to stroll on the beach by herself, dreaming. The sand, which a few hours before had burned the soles of her feet, was now like cool velvet. She walked down to the water's edge and then headed toward the jetty. The couple was gone. She was alone on the beach except for the gulls and the scurrying sandpipers.

With each step she dug a foot into the heavy, damp sand and then lifted it up to watch her footprint fill with water and disappear. Sometimes when she saw a tiny breathing hole form as the surf retreated, she knelt and scooped out the sand with her hands, looking for sand crabs. Far away she could hear unseen children shouting. The only other sounds were of waves crashing and birds screeching.

She stood up and faced the water. Beyond the breakers, gulls floated serenely on the billows. They were an audience.

Clutching an imaginary microphone with her right hand and gesturing with the left, she began to sing at the top of her lungs. She was Serena Sue Miletta, performing a concert in the stadium at the Meadowlands. The surf's roar was actually thunderous applause. Her backup group withdrew, leaving her alone with her fans. She smiled at them graciously and bowed her head, her arms outstretched, her fingers still curled around the make-believe mike.

"Sally! What on earth are you doing?"

Her face, her arms, her legs tingled with embarrassment. She turned and saw that Miranda had come up behind her, noiseless as a cat. "Nothing," she muttered.

"You must have been doing something. I saw you from the deck. It looked like you were praying or something."

"Did anyone else see me?"

"No. The grown-ups were too busy talking, and the kids were too busy playing cards."

Sally collapsed on the sand like a rag doll. She had to tell Miranda something. She might as well tell her the truth. "If you must know, I was singing."

"I like to sing too," Miranda said.

"That's nice," Sally said. Some response was required, and she couldn't think of a better one.

"I'm a very good singer."

Wouldn't you know. "I'm a very good singer too," Sally returned coldly.

Miranda crouched in the sand. "Yes," she said. "I've heard."

"Who told you?"

"Your mom wrote my mom about your solo in your school's Winter Concert. I'm probably not as good as you."

Sally melted a little. "You won't tell them, will you? I mean about the bowing."

"Of course not." Miranda sounded insulted. "What do you think I am, some kind of tattletale?"

That's exactly what Sally did think. But she didn't say so. "Sometimes," she remarked instead, "I imagine that I'm a big rock star singing a concert or something. You know, like Serena Sue Miletta."

Miranda nodded, her large blue-green

eyes serious and sympathetic. Aunt Nan was right about one thing—Miranda was certainly pretty. Beautiful, in fact. "I love Serena Sue Miletta," she said. "She's in Atlantic City now."

Sally nodded. "She's starring in *Carnival* at the Bellevue."

"I wish I could go. But my mother hates Atlantic City."

"Like my father." Sally felt a momentary urge to tell Miranda about the trip the Four Seasons were planning. But like the itch of her mosquito bites, it soon passed.

"I'm sure I'd love Atlantic City. I love lots of things my mother hates. We're so different. She can't draw. She can't sing."

"My folks are both absolutely tone deaf," Sally commented.

Miranda didn't reply. For a moment longer, they sat in silence, staring at the sea. The wind blew in gusts from the north, and Miranda, wearing only shorts and a tube top, shivered. "Maybe we'd better go back," she said. "Maybe they're getting ready to eat."

Sally glanced up toward the house. She

could see figures moving about on the deck. Her mother was carrying a tray inside. Aunt Nan, Rhoda, and Lenny were leaning over the table, probably setting it. Sally rose to her feet. "Yeah," she said. "I guess they are."

Miranda stood up too, and then, at the same moment, they both saw the woman who was approaching them from the direction of the jetty. She waved at them and shouted, "Wait. Wait for me."

"I wonder what she wants," Sally said.

Miranda shrugged and shook her head.

Though she was short, scarcely taller than they were, the woman's long, athletic stride brought her to them in a moment. Why had she hailed them? Sally had never ever seen her before in her life. If she had, she would have remembered.

The woman wasn't young. She was as old as Aunt Nan, at least. Sally could tell that from her lined brown skin. But her short wavy hair was dyed a brilliant orange, and her blue eyes were as bright as a baby's. Huge gold hoops dangled from her ears, and she was dressed in an ankle-length terry-cloth muumuu striped in brilliant slashes of pink, yellow, and the same shade of orange as her hair. "Hello, Sally," she said. "Hello, Miranda."

Sally was so surprised at the woman's use of their names that she uttered exactly the words she was thinking. "We don't know you. How do you know us?"

The woman's face wrinkled with laughter. "I'm Tanya," she said. "I'm a witch."

"That explains everything," Sally replied, wrinkling her nose.

"You don't believe in witches?" Tanya inquired.

"She didn't say that," Miranda interposed hastily.

"Miranda, darling, don't worry," Tanya said in a soothing voice, "I won't do anything bad to your cousin. I'm not that kind of witch."

"Thank goodness!" Sally's voice dripped disbelief.

"We have to go up to supper now," Miranda said politely. "Is there something you want?"

"Oh, no. I came out to hunt for shells

and watch the moon rise. I thought you might keep me company."

"That sounds nice," Sally said. "But we do have to go."

"I'll be here tomorrow night, just a little bit later. Maybe you'll be done with dinner by then. If you come, I'll show you something special. I mean, besides the moon."

"We'll come if we can," Miranda said. "So long, Tanya."

"Good-bye," Sally added. The two of them turned and started up the beach. When she was sure they were out of Tanya's earshot, Sally glanced back over her shoulder and then said, "You can meet her tomorrow night if you want to, but you shouldn't have said I would come."

"Don't you want to?"

"Well, no, I don't think so."

"Why not?"

Sally paused and turned so that she faced Miranda. "Have you seen Tanya before?"

Miranda nodded.

"So that's how she knew our names."

Miranda nodded again.

"So she's no witch."

"Yes, she is," Miranda insisted. "If you come tomorrow, you'll see that she is. She can do all kinds of things."

"Not magic."

Miranda frowned and kicked at the sand with her toe. And then, suddenly noticing something, she knelt and reached for it. "Look, Sally. Look what I found." She held up a large snail shell.

Sally took the shell in her hand and turned it over and over, examining it like a jeweler looking at a diamond through his glass. It was whole and perfect. To find one without damage of any kind was rare. To find one so far up the beach was rarer still.

Sally turned toward the ocean. Tanya still stood at the edge, but now her back was to the water. She raised her hand and waved.

Miranda waved back. Then, slowly, Sally lifted her arm and waved too.

Sally carried the snail shell the rest of the way home, but when they reached the house, she handed it back to Miranda. "How do you know this Tanya?" she asked.

"I've met her twice before," Miranda replied. "On the beach, at this same time. You know, like twilight. Both times we've found beautiful shells, really unusual ones, nothing like the broken old things I pick up when I'm alone." She opened her fist and gazed at the shell in her palm. "You could have this," she offered. "I have so many. You could have it if you wanted it."

Sally shook her head. "No, you found it, you keep it. Maybe," she added casually, "maybe if I don't have anything to do tomorrow night, maybe I will come here with you. We'll see."

After dinner, they all cleared the table, and then the Berg parents and Aunt Nan did the dishes. The others were excused. "Three people is enough of a crowd in a little kitchen," said the twins' mother. "The rest can take turns other nights."

Even though the moonlight made a shining silver path on the water, Lenny soon grew visibly bored sitting on the deck. "I'm going home," he said. "I want to watch the ball game. Coming, Rhoda?"

"Yeah," she said. "Sure."

"How about Miranda?" Jenny asked. "Is she going with you?"

"She can stay," Lenny said. "She can play with you guys. I'll come back for her later."

"We're not going to do anything," Emily said. "We're tired. We're going to bed."

Who went to bed at nine o'clock on vacation? Rhoda's quizzical glance made it clear she suspected Emily was lying. But Miranda said, "I'm tired too. I'm going home with you."

Sally glanced at her. Her face was closed, expressionless. *I should say something,* Sally thought. *I should tell her we're going to the Frosted Mug. Maybe I should even tell her about Atlantic City.* But really, she didn't want to. She drew her lips together in a tight line.

The grown-ups clattered down the steps, Miranda pattering silently behind them. Jake went inside. In a little while he came out again. "It's all set," he said. "Aunt Nan's going to the Mug with us so we can have our Four Seasons meeting there." With so much company, the house was too crowded for a meeting. Outdoors, with the moon shining, it was light enough, but too cool to sit on the deck or the beach. They felt like eating ice cream anyway.

Walking over, they sang the Four Seasons Anthem, composed by Sally months before to the tune of the Notre Dame Fight Song.

> For Jenny and Jake let's give a
>   cheer,
> Emmy and Sally are also right
>   here,
> Always loyal, always friends,
> We'll stick together till the end.
> Aunt Nanny feeds us both day
>   and night,
> We're full of spaghetti, power,
>   and might.
> You can't break us up—we'll tell
>   you why:
> We're the Four Seasons; we never
>   say die.

"We sound like a bunch of crows," Aunt Nan said. "Except for Sally, of course."

"Not really," Sally disagreed. "And with

a little practice, you'd sound a lot better. I mean, we've sung songs in our plays. They weren't so bad."

"They're always very short," Jenny pointed out. "Nanny makes sure of that."

At the Mug they carried cones and sundaes over to an empty picnic table on the floodlit cement patio. Aunt Nan smacked her lips over coffee ice cream, hot fudge, wet nuts, and whipped cream. "I needed a fix," she said. "Not a dollop of ice cream in either of your houses. Your parents are always on diets. I was suffering withdrawal."

"Let's stick to the agenda," Emily said. "We're here to talk about Atlantic City. We could put on a play, the way we do, only this time we could charge."

"It's hard to charge for something you usually do for free," Jake said.

"How about a concert?" Sally suggested.

"You heard Aunt Nan," Jenny reminded her. "Except for you, we're crows."

"Miranda's not a crow."

"Miranda's not one of the Four Seasons either," Jenny snapped.

"I wish she were," Aunt Nan said.

"There's no such thing as five seasons," Emily commented.

"You could change the name," Aunt Nan suggested.

Her remark was ignored. "How do you know Miranda's not a crow?" Jake asked.

"She told me," Sally replied.

"Because she said it, does that make it true?"

"Even if Miranda can sing, we can't have a concert," Emily said. "Two people are not enough for a concert."

"You can manage to sing something," Sally said. "You can all carry a tune. The three of you can be like a chorus in the background."

"Absolutely not," Jake said. "I won't sing. Not even in the chorus. Not even in the background."

Sally knew how Jake felt about singing. Just a few months before, he'd actually refused to participate in the school's Winter Concert, the one in which she'd had a solo. But she tried to persuade him anyway. "Jake, no one would really care. It would be our family. They would think we were wonderful no matter what we sounded like."

"We couldn't make enough money off just the family," Emily pointed out.

"I won't sing," Jake insisted. "And I mean it."

"Jake, I can't stand it, you're so stubborn."

"Listen, Sally," Emily chimed in, "it isn't just Jake. The rest of us don't want to sing either. We have to think of something else."

"You have to make a budget first," Aunt Nan said.

"What do you mean, a budget?" asked Emily.

"Figure out how much a trip to Atlantic City will cost you. Until you know that, you really don't know where you stand."

Emily nodded slowly. "You're right," she said.

Jenny clapped her hand on Emily's shoulder. "I appoint you to find out how much money we'll need," she said. Jenny was the new president of the Four Seasons, having been elected to that exalted office at the May meeting. "Once Emily tells us what we need, we can figure out how to get it," she announced. "Meeting adjourned."

Emily spent the next morning on the telephone. By the time they gathered on Jenny and Jake's deck to eat their lunch, she was able to announce the result of her research. "Round trip on the Black Whale is fifteen dollars for children under twelve. Admission to the performance of *Carnival* at the Bellevue is ten dollars each. I talked to Lisa. Dinner at the Seafood Garden runs about fifteen dollars a person, including a tip. It's lucky we don't drink. If we did, dinner would cost twice as much."

"Lucky they won't let us gamble either," Jenny remarked.

"We could eat in a cheaper place," Jake suggested. "We could eat at Burger King."

"That's no fun," Sally said. "We always eat at Burger King."

"We'll need extra money," Jenny said, "to spend on the boardwalk."

"Well, I think that could be up to each of us individually," Emily said. "That doesn't have to be a group expense." She looked down at the paper in front of her. "It comes to one hundred sixty dollars."

Sally whistled through her teeth. She couldn't imagine four kids under twelve coming up with that much money in a thousand years.

"Even if we did eat at Burger King, we'd still need about a hundred and thirty," Jake said.

"What difference does it make, really?" Sally said. "A hundred and thirty, a hundred and sixty, two hundred—it's all equally impossible."

"And we haven't even counted Aunt Nan," Emily pointed out. "She'll have to pay for herself."

"Hopeless," Jake said. "Absolutely hopeless."

"I think it's much too soon to give up," Jenny exclaimed. "We have to think. We have to spend the whole afternoon thinking. We'll meet again later and see what we've come up with."

"We all have *some* money," Emily said. "We could start with that."

"That's a good beginning." Jenny nodded her approval.

"I need my money," Jake said. "I'm saving to buy videos of old comedians. You know, Abbott and Costello and Laurel and Hardy and guys like that. Hey, Sally, who's on first? . . ."

Sally grinned, but shook her head without replying. She wasn't going to be caught in one of the comic routines Jake had memorized, even though by now she knew quite a few of them by heart herself.

"Hey, look," Emily cried. She leaned over the railing and pointed down the beach. The others turned to gaze in the same direction. A figure coming from the south plowed through the sand, a fair, slender girl in a flowered bathing suit.

"The Whiner," Jake said.

"Let's get out of here," Jenny said. "Fast."

"Where?" Emily asked. "Not the beach."

"The playground."

"I'm going to the library," Sally said. "I've got books to return. They're due today. I can't waste Atlantic City money on fines."

"If you don't hurry, she'll catch you," Jenny warned.

"You want to come with me, Emily?" Sally asked.

But Emily, already halfway down the stairs, seemed not to have heard. Jake and Jenny followed her, and Sally trailed slowly behind. *I don't care,* she thought. *Let Miranda find me. I'll just tell her I can't go to the beach because I have to go to the library. And if she says she wants to come, I'll tell her she can't because I'm riding my bike. And if she says she'll go home and get her bike, well then, let her, because it's a free country, and she can go to the library too if she wants to.*

But Sally didn't have to say any of those things because Miranda never turned up. Perhaps it hadn't been Miranda walking on the beach after all. Lots of blonde girls had flowered bathing suits.

Sally fetched her books from the house, mounted her bike, and rode to the library. Jenny, Emily, and Jake were still not back by the time she returned home. She considered biking over to the playground to find them, but it seemed unlikely they were still there. That hot, dusty, poorly equipped playground didn't have enough on it to occupy them for more than half an hour.

Though Sally wondered momentarily where the others might be, the brightly colored book jackets were calling to her. She selected *A Little Princess* by Frances Hodgson Burnett. Frances Hodgson Burnett almost always wrote about orphans. Sally carried the book out to the deck, where she lay down on a chaise, put on her sunglasses, and started to read. She'd wait for the kids to come back and then go down to the beach with them.

But they never returned. At first she scarcely noticed. The book was one of the best orphan stories she'd ever read. It wasn't until she'd finished it that she realized it had grown quite late. She went inside for a Kleenex with which to wipe her eyes and blow her nose. She glanced at the kitchen clock. It was almost five. Empty and silent, the house drowsed in the heat of the afternoon sun. Sally didn't want to stay there any longer. She wanted to go swimming, and swimming, unlike reading, was not something she liked to do alone. She wished Jenny, Emily, and Jake would come home.

Chomping on an apple, she wandered back out onto the deck, and saw them down below, leaning their bikes against the house. "Where have you been?" she called. "I was waiting for you."

Emily was the first one up the stairs. Her hair was plastered to her scalp, and patches of dampness darkened the T-shirt she wore over her bathing suit. "You were swimming!" Sally accused.

"Yes, at the end of the island," Emily replied. "The beach is wonderful there, so wide."

"I know. Why didn't you come get me?"

Jenny and Jake plopped down side by side on a chaise. "We did come back," Jake said, "to get our bikes. But you weren't here."

"I only went to the library," Sally protested. "You could have waited a couple more minutes."

"No, we couldn't," Jenny said. "Matron was going to lock us in the orphanage cellar, for punishment. We had to get away."

"We found out why our parents left us with such a terrible person in the first place," Emily said.

"Without me? You found that out without me?" Sally shouted.

"Shh!" Jake warned. "Matron pretended to be a long-lost aunt. That's how she fooled the mother and father. They worked for the government, and they left us with her when they were sent on a secret space mission. The capsule crashed."

"You mean they're really dead? We know that for sure now?" Sally whispered.

"No, of course not," Jenny exclaimed.

"The game would be over if we knew that," said Emily.

"Not necessarily." Sally sighed and shook her head. "I can't believe you guys played the Orphan Game without me." She played it without them all the time, inside her own head, but when she did, she made sure nothing important happened.

"We were afraid Miranda might show up," Emily explained.

"Well, she didn't. That wasn't her you saw on the beach. It was someone else."

"She still could have shown up. Later."

"What are we going to do?" Sally wondered. "Spend the rest of the month avoiding Miranda?"

"It's fun," Jake said.

Sally gazed at Jake. "Fun for you," she snapped. "Not for Miranda."

Jenny lifted her head and stared at Sally. "What's gotten into you?" she asked. "Why are you such a fan of Miranda's, all of a sudden?"

"I'm not a fan of hers," Sally said. "I don't like her any more than you do. But that's no reason to act like she has cooties or something. I mean, she isn't a criminal. She's our *cousin.*"

"Saint Sally," Jenny retorted with a lift of her eyebrows.

"That's an awful thing to say about me," Sally protested. "Just awful."

"That you're a saint?" Jenny began to laugh. "I didn't know it was an insult."

Emily and Jake added their laughter to hers. For a moment, Sally's sharp eyes shot sparks at the three of them. Then, suddenly, she began to laugh too.

"Come on," Jenny said. "There's still time for another swim before supper." She leaped to her feet and started down the stairs. The others followed, Sally bringing up the rear, her step slow, her eyes thoughtful.

She hated it when there was a quarrel among the Four Seasons. She was glad the little storm had passed. But she was possessed of the uncomfortable suspicion that like the island's winds, it might blow up again at any time.

Three

The grown-ups went out for dinner. On their way, Lenny and Rhoda dropped Miranda at the twins' house. Eight kids sat around the big table in the Bergs' front room and ate the tuna casserole and salad the twins' mother had left for them. Silently, Miranda shoveled food into her mouth. Perhaps because they'd been spared her company all day, no one teased her, but no one spoke to her either, not even Sally, though she occasionallly glanced in her direction. Miranda seemed always to be looking at her plate.

For dessert, Lisa passed around a box of Popsicles specially purchased for the occasion. When it finally reached her, Miranda peered inside the package. "I don't like lemon Popsicles, and I don't like strawberry Popsicles. I only like orange Popsicles."

"That's too bad," Lisa said. "The orange Popsicles are all gone."

Emily and Jake were unwrapping orange Popsicles. "Will one of you trade with me?" Miranda asked.

Emily shook her head. "Why should we?" Jake asked. "We like orange best too."

"But lemon and strawberry make me sick." Miranda's voice rose to a high-pitched whine. "I bet they don't make you sick."

"I don't intend to find out," Jake retorted.

"You should be nicer to me," Miranda said. "I came all the way from Colorado to be with you." Obviously she was echoing some remark of her parents'. Anyone with half a brain would have known enough not to repeat it.

"I didn't invite you," Jake said. "None of us did."

"Your parents did."

"That's their business," Emily returned grimly.

Miranda looked as if she were going to cry. Then a sudden thought appeared to distract her. She pushed away from the table and hurried outside. A moment later, she opened the screen door and poked her head back in. "You coming with me, Sally?" she called.

Sally frowned in puzzlement.

Without a word, Miranda reached into her pocket and pulled out the snail shell.

"Oh. Now I remember," Sally replied quietly. "No, I'm not coming with you."

Disappointment showed in Miranda's face, but, saying no more, she let go of the screen door. It slammed, and she disappeared down the steps.

"Where did she want you to go?" Jenny asked.

"Just for a walk, to look for shells." Sally didn't mention Tanya. If the others found out that Miranda believed she'd met a witch on the beach, their hoots would be so loud they'd blow her all the way back to Denver.

The grown-ups had left behind two dollars for each kid. Chip, Lisa, and Amy had decided to spend their money at a video game parlor. "We'll walk over with you," Jake said. "We're going on the rides."

"Wait!" Emily raised her hand like a traffic cop. "Let's play miniature golf instead. One game'll last a lot longer than four rides, and it'll only cost a dollar." Her voice was heavy with significance. "Then we'll each have a dollar left."

Jake knew what she was driving at. "Four dollars won't get us to At—"

"Shut up!" Jenny slapped her hand over Jake's mouth. The Big Kids were not ever supposed to know what the Four Seasons were planning. It was written in the constitution.

But the Big Kids were too busy debating which game parlor to patronize to pay any attention to what the Little Kids were talking about—not, Sally thought, that they cared much anyway.

"Listen, Jake, you have to start somewhere," Jenny whispered. "Four dollars is a beginning."

The Big Kids were on their way out the door when suddenly Chip turned back. "Hey, you guys," he said, "wherever you go, take Miranda with you. Don't leave her out on the beach alone." And then the three of them were gone.

"He's right," Sally said. "If we ran out on her, the parents would kill us when they got back."

"She's his cousin too," Jenny complained. "Why doesn't *he* take her with him?"

"That'll be the day," Sally groaned. She pulled two crumpled dollar bills out of the pocket of her shorts and handed them to Emily. "Here. Start the Atlantic City Fund with this. I'm going to stay home and read. When Miranda comes back, I'll be here."

"I'll save it up in my bureau drawer," Emily said. "In a sock." She pulled out one of her own dollar bills and added it to the two Sally had given her. "Now one from you and you," she said to Jenny and Jake. They each handed theirs over, and Emily trotted off to the bedroom to stash them away.

Jake turned to Sally. "Thanks."

"For what?"

"For hanging around so the grown-ups won't bite our heads off if Miranda tells them we left her alone, which she surely would."

"Sally's a saint," Jenny said. "We all know that."

Sally flushed uncomfortably. This was the second time in one day Jenny had called her a saint, and she still didn't like it. "I'm not staying home to be nice. I *hate* miniature golf. I actually hate it." She always lost at miniature golf, just as she always lost at hearts. "And I love to read."

"I always knew you loved to read," Jenny said. "But I never knew you hated miniature golf."

"Well, I never mentioned it before."

Jenny raised her eyebrows. "That's what I mean. You're a saint."

When Emily returned from the bedroom, she, Jake, and Jenny left. Sally spread out her library books on the coffee table, trying to make up her mind which one to start. She picked up a volume, stared at its cover, put it down again, and then did the same with another and another. Between herself and the books, an image seemed to interpose itself, an image with orange hair and gold hoops in its ears. Suddenly, impatiently, she pushed the books into a pile and hurried out of the house, down the steps, and over the dunes to the beach. The sky above the ocean was dark, but behind her, rimming the bay, the western horizon glowed red and gold. She was able to see well enough to avoid falling into holes, and well enough to make out human shapes in the distance, but not well enough to identify them. Twice, by the water's edge, she thought she'd come upon Miranda and Tanya, only to realize, when she got close, that she'd been mistaken.

She walked quickly, hoping to find them before the light was entirely gone. By the time she reached the jetty, it was too dark to risk a climb over slippery, damp rocks.

She trotted back up the beach to make her way across at the point where the stones were buried by drifting sand.

I'm Julia, she thought, *the orphan Julia. Marchmain, Octavia, and Juliette have stowed away on a freighter to escape Matron's clutches, but I have insisted on remaining behind to confront the mysterious lady with the orange hair, because I'm sure that concealed in a seashell she holds the secret of our royal identity. I have disguised myself as plain old Sally Berg and taken shelter with a perfectly ordinary family who have no notion that I'm actually a princess. But the lady with the orange hair knows. She's a witch and she sees through my cover to the truth.*

A gust of wind prickled the skin on Sally's face and ruffled her hair. She thought she heard a sound borne on the breeze, thin, silvery music, like bells. She paused for a moment, listening. Fortunately, the tide was out, and the crash of the surf didn't drown out all other noises. Yes, now she was sure. She heard bells, and voices too, tinkling, wordless voices.

She started up the beach. The farther she got from the sea, the sharper the sounds became. She realized she wasn't hearing bells at all, but wind chimes. They grew clearer and clearer, and so did the voices, two voices, the voices of a woman and a girl.

A pair of figures perched high above the sand on a lifeguard stand. "Hello, Sally," one of them called out.

Though she'd heard that voice only once before, on the previous evening, Sally recognized its peculiar husky tones. "Hello, Tanya," she said.

"I'm glad you came after all," Miranda said. "We're having such a nice time."

"Much too fine a night to stay in," Tanya said. "The moon will be up in a minute. We're singing moon songs. Won't you sing with us?"

"I don't know any moon songs," Sally replied.

"Of course you do. Shove over, Miranda. There's room for Sally if we squeeze."

Sally mounted the rungs on the side of the stand and climbed into the seat next to Miranda. Her hand knocked against bamboo chimes suspended from a crossbar, causing a sudden burst of rippling sound. "I brought them with me," Tanya explained. "I like to hear the wind, especially when I'm watching the moon rise. See? There it comes."

The edge of the moon gleamed on the horizon. Tanya began to sing.

> By the light of the silvery moon
> I want to spoon,
> To my honey I'll croon love's
>   tune . . .

Sally had never heard the song before. Miranda probably hadn't either. It was not one of the top ten. But the tune was so simple that in a few moments the two of them were singing along, at first hesitantly, but then full-voiced, as if they were all on the stage performing at a concert.

> Honeymoon keep a-shining in June,
> Your silv'ry beams
> Will bring love dreams,
> We'll be cuddling soon
> By the silvery moon.

Tanya taught them other songs too, like "Moon River" and "Blue Moon" and "Moon over Miami" and "Moonlight in Vermont" and "Shine on Harvest Moon." As they sang, the moon, like a huge white cookie, rose higher and higher in the sky, until Sally could see Tanya's orange hair and striped caftan almost as clearly as if it were day. The wind chimes tinkled. Sally realized she did indeed know some moon songs. In her clear, powerful voice, she began to sing one from her Serena Sue Miletta tape.

> Moonlight madness,
> Lunacy—
> What crazy things
> Are you doing to me?

At first, Miranda just listened, her eyes intent on Sally's face. Then she joined in. Their voices soared through the darkness, until the moon itself seemed to smile down at them. Accompanied by Miranda's perfect harmony, Sally felt as if she could reach up and grab stars by the handful.

When the song was over, there was silence for a moment. Tanya sighed, and then, with rhythmic claps, applauded. "That's a good song. A very good song." She kissed Miranda's cheek, and then she kissed Sally's. "It's getting late now. You'd better go back. The moon is so bright you won't have any trouble seeing your way. If you meet me tomorrow, I'll show you something wonderful."

"You were supposed to show us something wonderful today," Sally remembered.

"I did."

"What was that?"

"The moon music, of course. Yesterday the snail shell, today the moon music."

Sally had come down out of the sky. "You didn't make up those songs."

"I didn't make up the snail shell either."

"You're not really a witch."

"She is, she is," Miranda insisted.

"I've changed my mind about tomorrow," Tanya said. "I won't show you something wonderful. We'll *do* something wonderful. It'll have to be during the day, though."

66

"Where should we come?" Miranda asked. "And when?"

"Two-eighty-nine Pearl Street," Tanya replied. "Ten o'clock in the morning." Grasping the wind chimes in one hand and the side rail of the chair in the other, she swung herself over as easily as if she were no older than the girls, and dropped to the ground with a gentle thud. "Good night, Miranda. Good night, Sally. Go home now, both of you. See you tomorrow." She strode away across the shadowy dunes. Sally could hear the wind chimes long after she'd lost sight of Tanya's retreating figure.

Sally dropped to the ground the way Tanya had. Miranda climbed down carefully, rung by rung. They walked back to the house on the hard, cold sand along the water's edge. "Will you come with me tomorrow?" Miranda asked.

Sally wanted to. People passing by on the beach who'd heard them singing night songs at the top of their lungs, like three dogs barking at the moon, must have thought they'd encountered three weirdos. It had been a crazy thing to do—but fun, lots of fun. So she was naturally curious as to what Tanya had in store for them the next day. "Do you think," she queried tentatively, "we should bring the others with us? Tanya doesn't seem the type who'd mind." Miranda was entitled to consultation on any issue involving Tanya. In a way, Tanya belonged to her.

"Well, we could ask them. I don't think they'll come."

"Of course they'll come. Why shouldn't they?"

"Because it's me."

"They're not going to give up an adventure just because they . . ." Sally found she couldn't finish the sentence.

"Just because they don't like me." Miranda finished it for her. "They will," she added with gloomy conviction.

They said little to each other the rest of the way home. It seemed to Sally that she was swimming in moonlight. Of course, she'd always known a full moon was beautiful. And a crescent moon too, and stars—all the night on the beach, where the bright lights of town could not obscure the natural lights of heaven. But she had never noticed the beauty so sharply before, never before felt as if she could touch it and taste it.

Back at the house, the grown-ups had returned from dinner and Jenny, Jake, and Emily from miniature golf. Only the Big Kids were still out. As Sally and Miranda came up the stairs, Lenny was pacing back and forth on the deck. "Oh, honey," he exclaimed when he saw Miranda, "thank goodness you're here. I was worried about you."

"We were only walking on the beach," Miranda said.

"Don't you think it was a little dangerous to do that alone at night? Suppose something happened to you?"

"We weren't alone," Miranda pointed out. "We were with each other." She didn't mention Tanya. "What do you think could happen to me down there? Did you think some humongous shark was going to walk up on the beach and gobble me up? Gobble *us* up," she corrected herself.

"Of course not, honey. Only nowadays

you can't be too careful. It's late, time for bed. We'll go home now. Don't worry your mother and me like this again."

"Mom wasn't worried," Miranda said. "I'm sure she wasn't." At that moment, Rhoda stepped out on the deck. "Were you, Mom?"

"Was I what?"

"Worried about me?"

"No," Rhoda said. "What for?"

"See, Dad? I told you so."

"She was worried," Lenny insisted. "She's just covering up."

"Me?" Rhoda returned with a small laugh. "I never cover anything up."

Miranda shot Sally an I-told-you-so glance. But Sally really wasn't sure what it meant. And since Miranda and her family departed immediately, she didn't have a chance to find out.

In their room, Sally and Emily prepared for bed. "Tomorrow morning we're going to have a Four Seasons meeting," Emily said. "Jenny insists she won't adjourn it until we've come up with a plan."

"Can't we meet in the afternoon?" Sally suggested.

"Why? What's wrong with the morning?"

"Miranda and I met this lady on the beach. We want to go over to her house tomorrow morning. We want you guys to come too."

"What kind of lady?"

"An old lady, with orange hair. I think we could put her in the Orphan Game. She knows things."

"Like what?"

"Things. She says she's a witch."

Emily stared at her. "You've gone off your rocker."

"*I* didn't say she's a witch. *She* says she's a witch."

"You want us to go visit some crazy old lady? What for?"

"She says we're going to do something wonderful."

"Like what?"

"I don't know. It's a surprise."

"You don't even know what we're going to do when we get there, but you want us to go?"

Sally leaned back against her pillow with a sigh. She hadn't said this right, not any of it. She tried again. "You can have a lot of fun with Tanya."

"Tanya?"

"That's her name, Tanya."

"What kind of fun?"

What, what, what. Was that the only word Emily knew? "Well," Sally tried to explain, "tonight Miranda and Tanya and I sat in one of the lifeguard stands and watched the moon come up and sang songs."

"Sounds terrific."

Sally felt that she could touch the sarcasm in Emily's voice. "It *was* fun," she replied defensively.

"You and I have different ideas of fun. I thought you were staying home to read."

"That's not your idea of fun either."

"At least it's normal."

"I got kind of worried about Miranda. I went out looking for her."

"Now you sound like Cousin Lenny. I think Miranda ought to start taking care of herself, whether Cousin Lenny likes it or not."

Sally didn't feel like defending Miranda. It was time to write down recent developments in the Orphan Game. She picked up the notebook and scribbled a paragraph describing the perfect snail shell that held the secret of the orphans' identity. Emily stood in front of the mirror and brushed her long sun-lightened hair a hundred strokes. Then she climbed into the double bed and lay with her back to Sally. After a while, Sally turned off the light. There was no further conversation.

Jenny biked to Jack's Bakery in the morning to buy a dozen sticky buns. She put the box in the middle of the table on her deck and brought out paper cups, paper napkins, and a half gallon of milk. Jake shouted across the narrow alley between the houses. "Emily and Sally, come on over. Breakfast meeting."

"Who do you think you are?" Lisa asked. "Company presidents?"

Sally hoped big executives came to a decision more easily than their club. The sticky buns were all gone, and the Four Seasons were still arguing. "Maybe we'd better postpone the trip to next summer," Emily suggested. "That'll give us all year to raise the money."

"The orphans have to go to Atlantic City," Sally announced suddenly. "There's this shell in one of the souvenir shops along the boardwalk. It contains the secret of their identity."

Jake nodded approvingly. "How did it get there?"

Sally decided to leave Tanya out of it. "Well, it was in the Denver Horror's suitcase when he arrived at the orphanage. He's got something to do with the orphans' real identity, though I don't know what. Miss Priss thought the shell was just a piece of junk, so she sold it along with a whole bunch of garbage at a garage sale."

"Well, maybe the orphans think they have to get to Atlantic City, and maybe the Four Seasons think they have to get to Atlantic City," Emily responded with her usual practicality, "but that does nothing to actually *get* any of them there."

For a moment, they were all silent, racking their brains. Jenny picked up her needlepoint and began to work it. "So this meeting won't be a total waste of time," she said.

Sally watched Jenny's needle dart swiftly in and out of the canvas. "Hey, you could sell that! You could make a lot of them and sell them."

"They take too long," Jenny said. "I've been working on this one for a week now, and it isn't even half done."

"But that's a good idea," Jake said. "An art sale. We could make pictures and decorate shells and stuff like that and sell it."

"Who would buy it, except our relatives?" Emily queried.

"Around here, that ought to be enough," Jake pointed out.

"We may not be able to get all of the money that way, but we can get some of it," Emily remarked. "We probably can't get all that we need by doing just one thing anyway."

At the head of the table, Jenny stood up. "We don't have time to wait around for the perfect plan. We'll start with an art sale. And we won't invite just our relatives. We'll invite everyone we know on the whole Long Beach Island." She spoke so authoritatively that the others simply nodded their agreement. "I've got paper and paints and crayons. We'll start right now. We'll work all day."

Jenny and Jake went inside the house to fetch the art supplies. By the time they returned, Miranda had ridden up on her bike.

She didn't come over to the table, but stood on the top step and spoke to Sally. "It's ten-fifteen. We better go."

"Sally's busy," Jenny said.

"But we have to go to Tanya's. She's expecting us."

"Who's Tanya?" Jake wondered.

While Sally was trying to think up a satisfactory way to explain Tanya, Emily answered for her. "This crazy old lady Miranda and Sally met on the beach."

"Let's all go to Tanya's house," Sally said brightly. "She wouldn't mind."

"We can't," Jenny said. "We have too much work to do."

"And besides, we don't even want to," Jake added.

"We'll have lots of fun." Sally hoped she sounded wonderfully persuasive. "We're going to do something special."

"Like what?" Jake asked.

"I don't know. It's a surprise."

Jake shook his head, sat down at the table, picked up a red crayon, and began to draw a picture of a castle. Forts and castles formed Jake's total artistic repertory.

"Please come, Sally," Miranda said. "Tanya is expecting you."

Sally faced Jenny. "I don't like drawing," she stated apologetically. "You know that."

"You don't like miniature golf. You don't like drawing. You don't like this. You don't like that." Jenny's voice was so low that only Sally could hear what she was saying. "What's gotten into you lately? You keep running out."

"I'll make it up to you, Jenny, really I will," Sally assured her. "I'll find some really good things to sell at the art show. Special shells and things—better than anything I could draw."

Jenny glanced at Miranda and returned her gaze to Sally. "I think you're starting to like Miranda better than you like us," she commented, her voice flat.

"Just because I don't hate her doesn't mean I like her better than I like you guys," Sally replied hotly. "I couldn't like anyone better than you. But I want to go to Tanya's. I promised."

"Well, go then," Jenny said. "See if I care." She sat down at the table and pulled a piece of paper toward her. Jake pushed aside the one he'd been working on and grabbed another.

"You're done already?" Emily asked.

Jake nodded.

Emily picked up the drawing and gazed at it. "You can't charge money for that. It's just a couple of lines."

"It'll only cost a quarter," Jake said.

"At that price we'll have to sell an awful lot of drawings."

"I can make an awful lot of drawings."

"But, Jake," Emily protested, "how many

crummy pictures of castles can one person buy?"

"Look, Emily," Jake explained patiently, "I can't draw good pictures. I can only draw crummy pictures. A lot of crummy pictures ought to be worth the same as a few good ones."

Jenny entered the argument on Emily's side. "They aren't. Five thousand scribbles doesn't equal one painting by Van Gogh."

"Ten thousand maybe?" Jake asked.

"Sally, I'm going now," Miranda said.

Jenny's attention had been diverted. It seemed a good moment to leave. Sally hurried down the stairs behind Miranda, who waited while she fetched her bike from the storage space under the house. They mounted up and pedaled down Beach Avenue toward Pearl Street.

In the center of Beach Haven, a collection of rambling Victorian structures had weathered more than a century of storms. Pearl Street was lined with such dwellings. Sally had walked or ridden by them a million times without paying them any particular attention.

But today she and Miranda rode slowly along the sidewalk inspecting the numbers on the front of each house. Two-eighty-nine turned out to be tall, narrow, and white, with two peaked dormers on the third floor. The wraparound porch was shaded by bright yellow awnings, and filled with pots of geraniums and philodendron and white wicker rocking chairs dressed up with yellow cushions.

Tanya was watering the plants. She wasn't wearing her striped caftan. She was wearing stained blue jeans and a sweatshirt. In the daytime she looked much less like a witch and much more like someone's grandmother, in spite of her orange hair.

She set down her watering can when she saw the girls on the front walk. "Touch late, aren't you? I was about to give up on you and get started myself."

"Sorry," Sally apologized. "There was a lot going on this morning."

"Too bad you didn't bring your sister and your cousins with you," Tanya said.

"They're busy."

"Well then, let's begin, before it gets too hot."

"What are we going to do?" Miranda asked.

"Come up here and I'll show you."

Tanya led them around to the side porch. Hanging on the wall was a large sculpture that looked like a mask made out of stone. Several similar, smaller pieces surrounded it. "We're going to make some more of these," Tanya said.

"Carve faces like this, out of stone?" Sally exclaimed. "I could never do that! I can't even draw."

"I *can* draw," Miranda said, "but I don't think I can carve, not anything so big, not out of stone."

Tanya grinned. "These are not carvings. They're not made out of stone. And they're much easier to do than you think."

Four

By the time Sally and Miranda re-mounted their bicycles for the ride home, it was three o'clock in the afternoon. They'd been with Tanya for more than four hours. Their clothes were covered with white plaster stains, but Tanya had assured them their shorts and tops would come as clean in the washing machine as their hair and skin had in the ocean.

They'd spent the morning making masks,

similar to the ones hanging on Tanya's porch, though of course not nearly as well done. Miranda's were good though, very good, Tanya had said, for a first-time effort. She'd praised Sally for trying. Sally had to admit that though the faces she'd created looked like creatures out of a nightmare, she'd had a wonderful time fooling around with wet sand and plaster, like a toddler with a pail and shovel baking sand cakes.

Lunch had been lovely too. They'd eaten on the porch, on a wicker table covered with an embroidered cloth. Tanya served them mushroom quiche, croissants, salad, linzer torte, and iced tea in long-stemmed goblets. Tanya cooked at least as well as Aunt Nan, possibly better.

"Can we come back tomorrow and sand cast some more?" Miranda asked.

"Not tomorrow," Tanya said. "It's going to rain tomorrow. Come the next day. Sunday, same time, same place."

Sally looked out at the cloudless blue sky. "The weatherman didn't say anything about rain on TV this morning. He said we were going to have a beautiful weekend."

"He's wrong, I'm right."

"How can you be so sure?" Sally wondered.

"I told you, I'm a witch."

This witch business had gone far enough. "You can't do magic, can you?" Sally phrased it as a question out of politeness.

"I can do some kinds of magic. I'm a sculptor. That's magic. All art is."

Miranda and Sally had been indoors to use the bathroom and help Tanya carry the food and dishes from the kitchen to the porch. The interior didn't look like a summer cottage. The white walls weren't hung with gift-shop posters, but with real paintings—oils and watercolors and acrylics. End tables bore figures cast in metal, mostly animals—a sleeping cat with his head in his paws, a horse leaping a fence, a tiger crouched and ready to spring.

"Who made this tiger?" Miranda had asked.

"I did," Tanya said. "I made all the animals."

"And the paintings?" Sally queried. "Did you do them too?"

"No. Look at them, really look at them. They're all in different styles. My paintings are upstairs, where no one can see them. Most of the ones down here were done by my boyfriends."

Sally smiled. She knew that Tanya was joking. People as old as Tanya didn't have boyfriends. Or maybe she was talking about the boyfriends she'd had when she was young.

Tanya pointed first to a still life, then to a seascape, and then to a brilliant orange and gold abstraction. "That's a Jean Claude. That's a Michael. That's an Antonio."

Sally enjoyed the pieces of sculpture even better than the paintings, and she enjoyed the linzer torte most of all. But neither the paintings, the sculpture, nor the food fit Sally's idea of magic. "You can't do real magic," she said. "You can't make something out of nothing."

"If what we did this morning wasn't making something out of nothing, than I don't know what is," Tanya retorted.

85

"What we did this morning was make something out of plaster, water, and sand," Sally said.

"But what we ended up with is nothing like plaster, water, and sand," Tanya insisted. She pointed to one of the faces Miranda had made, drying on a table in the sun. It was a king with a long nose, a beard, and a crown on his head. "If I said to you, 'That mask is plaster and sand,' what would I have told you about it, really? Nothing important."

Sally scratched her head. "I always thought magic was something you couldn't explain."

"Exactly," Tanya agreed. "And the world is full of things we can't explain. Well, maybe we can explain them, but our explanations don't tell us much. I mean, I know as well as you do what they teach you in school about the moon. It's made out of a lot of cold, dead rock. I know it shines only by light reflected from the sun. But to say that isn't to explain why I feel so wonderful when I watch the moon come up over the ocean. That's the magic."

86

"So what's a witch?" Sally asked.

"A witch is someone who can recognize magic when she sees it, and make use of it."

"Then anyone can be a witch."

"It takes training. But some people have a natural talent."

"Inherited, probably," Miranda said. "It must come through the genes."

Tanya smiled. "Maybe."

"Do you think I could be a witch?" Miranda asked hopefully. "Like you?"

Tanya was still smiling. "I'm sure you have the right genes. We can work on it."

Sally wondered if what Tanya had said about magic was true. Magic, imagination. Somehow, Tanya was saying, they went together. Sally knew she had plenty of imagination, but she wasn't at all sure that made her a witch—or made Miranda or Tanya witches either.

Later, biking along Beach Avenue, pedaling hard against a stiff wind out of the south, neither Sally nor Miranda had breath left for talking. When they arrived at Sally's house, they parked their bikes under the deck. "Now you believe Tanya's a witch, don't you?" Miranda asked.

"No more a witch than you or I."

Miranda sat down on the bottom step. "She's a witch. Today I found that out for sure."

"You did? How?"

"From what she said to me. About genes. She knows. I certainly never told her, and neither did anyone else. She just knows."

"Knows what?"

"That I'm an orphan."

"An orphan?" Sally cried. "What do you mean, an orphan? Cousin Lenny is your father, and Cousin Rhoda is your mother."

"I'm adopted."

"Yeah, I know." Sally plopped herself down next to Miranda, and thought for a minute. "But if you're adopted," she said at last, "an orphan is just what you're not. Not anymore. Lenny and Rhoda are your parents."

"Not my blood parents."

"Boy, no father could fuss over a kid more than Cousin Lenny fusses over you."

Miranda nodded. "He worries about me all right. They had their own little girl before they got me. She died."

Sally nodded. She knew that too. So did Emily, Jenny, and Jake. No one had ever discussed it with them directly, but the grown-ups talked and the kids overheard, even when they weren't actually listening. It was one of the things they just knew, had always known, and thought almost nothing about. It was sad that Lenny and Rhoda's little girl had died, but after all, they'd never met her.

Miranda was still talking. "Dad thinks maybe I'll die too, and he worries. He's just a worrier anyway. He'd worry over a dog. Of course, we don't have one, because he says maybe I'd be allergic to a dog. I love animals. They don't. That's another reason you can sure tell those two aren't my birth parents."

"You can?"

"It's obvious. We're so different. I mean, they're all right, I love them, but they don't understand me. They don't have the faintest idea of what's going on in my head."

"Whose mother and father do? Sometimes I feel as if my parents and I are perfect strangers."

From her pocket Miranda pulled the snail shell she'd found on the beach the night Sally had first met Tanya. "Rhoda could never be my real mother. My real mother must be someone—well, someone more like Tanya."

"Your real grandmother, you mean."

"Mother. People can have children late. Some people can even have them when they're forty-five. Maybe Tanya's my real mother."

"Come off it, Miranda."

"You never can tell." Miranda rolled the shell around in her hand as if it were a good luck charm. "Anyway, I know why you guys won't let me in."

"What guys?"

"What guys? What other guys are there? You and Emily and Jenny and Jake. It's because I'm not your real cousin. Not by blood."

With effort Sally resisted the impulse to take Miranda by the shoulders and shake her. "That is absolutely the dumbest thing I ever heard. You think every time we see you we say, 'Oh, here comes Miranda, she's adopted'? It never crosses our minds."

With her index finger, Miranda gently stroked the shell. "Then why *do* you shut me out?"

"Do we?" Sally replied. She was stalling for time. She couldn't say, *Because you whine and carry tales. Because we don't like you.* She just couldn't.

"You know you do. You've got a wall around you, the four of you. You won't let anyone in."

"We have lots of other friends at home."

"Maybe you do. But here at the beach, it's you four, period."

With the toe of her flip-flop, Sally drew circles in the gravelly yellow dirt. "Emily and I have two best friends at school, Petey and Gloria. Last year, they were mad at us for two weeks. They were calling Emily 'cootie girl,' and because I'm Emily's twin, they wouldn't speak to me. It was awful."

"But still, you had Emily."

"Yes. I always have Emily."

"And Jenny. And Jake."

"We fight a lot, all of us."

"But you still have them."

Sally didn't deny it. It was the truth.

"Do me a favor," Miranda added.

"If I can."

"Don't say anything about this to the others."

"About what?"

"About how I feel. About being left out. Keep it secret."

"Why did you tell me?"

"Because you're really not like them. You're sort of nice to me. I think—well, I think you're sort of my friend."

If Miranda thought Sally was her friend, she didn't expect much from friendship. "I won't tell," Sally promised. "It'll be hard, but I won't tell."

"OK, then," Miranda said.

Sally rose to her feet. "I have to find them now. They must be wondering where I am."

Miranda stood up too. "I'll go home. Mom and Dad are probably on the beach."

Sally looked away. "You don't have to

go home. You can stay here." She hoped Miranda would turn down the invitation guilt had forced her to issue.

But she was not surprised by Miranda's prompt response. "OK," Miranda said. "I'll stay."

The Berg house was deserted. Sally and Miranda found the house next door empty too. Sheets of paper covered the dining table. The two girls leafed through them, gazing at innumerable careless drawings of castles and forts. Emily's weren't much better, though they tended to depict flower gardens and houses rather than the history of military architecture.

Sally studied a pencil drawing of a shack alongside a railroad track, recognizing a pale imitation of a similar scene painted by Jenny which hung in her bedroom at home. "Scribble, scribble, scribble," Sally commented derisively. "They got bored. They wanted to get to the beach. Even Jenny got bored." She lay the drawing down on top of the others. "Jenny should do sand castings. She'd really enjoy doing them, and they'd be something worth selling."

"Selling?" Miranda queried. "What do you mean?"

"Our club is having an art show."

"Your club?"

"The Four Seasons. It's a private club."

"Private, of course."

Sally ignored that. "We're having an art show to raise money."

Miranda picked up one of Jake's drawings, stared at it, and put it down again. "Can I be in your art show?"

"I don't know."

"The Four Seasons can have the money you get selling my things."

Miranda was pleading. Sally felt her face flush with embarrassment. "It's all right with me," she said. "But we'll have to ask the others."

"Let's go find them," Miranda said.

But they weren't on the beach. The grown-ups were, but not the Big Kids, nor Emily, Jenny, or Jake. "Where are they?" Sally asked her mother.

"Crabbing, in the bay. They walked over after lunch."

"The Big Kids *and* the Little Kids?"

Her mother nodded.

"How come?"

Her mother shrugged. "Chip asked them to come along."

The first time in living memory such a thing had happened, and Sally had missed it! If she were Miranda, it would have been enough to make her cry. Instead, lips pressed tightly together, she threw herself face down on the sand, not even bothering to spread out her towel.

Miranda knelt at her side. "Sally! What's the matter?"

Sally lifted her head. "I missed it," she whispered fiercely. "The one time the Big Kids were willing to do something with us, I wasn't here. And crabbing too. I've never been crabbing."

"Who'd want to eat a crab?" Miranda said, making a face. "It'd be like eating a spider."

"Eating them isn't the point. Catching them is."

"But you and I had fun!" Miranda said.

"Not as much fun as crabbing."

"How do you know, if you've never been crabbing?"

"Oh, Miranda, anything with the Big Kids is more fun than . . ." Her voice trailed off. She put her head back down in the sand.

"More fun than being with me," Miranda finished.

"More fun than anything the Four Seasons does alone," Sally corrected sharply. "Listen, Miranda, I wish you'd stop feeling sorry for yourself."

"You don't know what it's like, being adopted," Miranda retorted. "You don't know what it's like, not knowing who your mother and father *really* are."

Sally sat up and took a deep breath. "I'm going to tell you something, Miranda. It's a secret, like the one you told me. Do you promise you won't tell a single, solitary soul?"

Solemnly, Miranda nodded.

"We play a game," Sally said. "Jenny, Jake, Emily, and me. We call it the Orphan Game. We pretend we don't know who our parents are, or where they are, or even if they're alive or dead. We have all kinds of adventures trying to escape from the orphanage and find them."

"That's the sickest game I ever heard of," Miranda exclaimed.

"Well, we don't think so. We read books about orphans, all the time. Especially me. We *love* orphans."

"That's because you've never been one."

"Neither have you. Not really."

"I don't know who my real parents are. That makes me an orphan." Miranda reached into her beach bag, pulled out her needlepoint and stitched at it savagely.

"You don't understand," Sally said.

"*You* don't understand," Miranda retorted.

Sally could see no point in pursuing the conversation. From her own bag, she retrieved the book she was reading. Losing herself in the story, she forgot about orphans, Miranda, the Big Kids, the Little Kids, and the crabs until, at the end of a chapter, she looked up and realized that her sister and cousins were on Jenny's deck, fussing with buckets. "I'm going up," Sally said. "I want to see what they caught."

"Me too." Instantly, Miranda leaped to her feet.

On the deck, Emily was kneeling by a pail, staring into its depths. "I think I'll keep one of them, for a pet," she said.

"Crabs make crummy pets," Jake informed her. "They don't *do* anything."

"This little one." Emily jabbed her finger into the water. "He's not worth cooking. There's nothing to him."

"I don't see how you can eat any of them," Miranda said. Now she too was staring into the bucket. "It would make me vomit."

"If you've never tasted one," Jenny said, "how do you know? Actually, crabs are delicious."

Jake reached into the bucket, grabbed a crab, and waved it in Miranda's face. "See? See the lovely crab?"

Screeching, Miranda retreated back against the railing. "I hope he grabs you with his claws," she yelled. "I hope he takes your nose off."

"He'll take yours off first," Jake said.

"Oh, Jake, don't be an idiot," Jenny scolded. "That crab will get you before he gets Miranda. Put him back."

Grinning, Jake obeyed. "Where're the Big Kids?" Sally wondered. "Mom said you went crabbing with them."

"They ran into Dave and Monty Schreiber," Jenny explained. "They decided to swim with them in the bay, so they told us to bring the crabs home."

"And you listened to them?" Sally made no effort to conceal her amazement.

"Before we even left, we had to promise to do just what they told us. Otherwise, they wouldn't have let us come." Jenny lifted her chin. "We had fun anyway. A lot of fun."

Sally eyed the crabs crawling under and over each other in the bottom of the bucket. "I wish I'd been with you."

"You could have been," Jenny replied coolly. "It was your choice."

Sally glanced at Jenny, and then turned away. "We had fun too."

"But you left us with all the work. We

didn't go crabbing until we'd made hundreds of pictures." *Hundreds of* lousy *pictures,* Sally thought. "We deserved to go crabbing," Jenny continued. "It was our reward for working so hard."

"We made things for the art show too," Sally said.

"You did?" Surprise replaced superiority in Jenny's voice.

"We made sand castings."

"We're going to make more on Sunday," Miranda chimed in. "You can come too," she added, as if conferring a great honor. "Tanya invited you."

"Wait a minute," Emily ordered. "What has this art show got to do with you, Miranda?"

"Sally said I can be in it. I'm good at art."

"I didn't say you could be in it," Sally corrected sharply. "I said I'd *ask* if you could be in it." She turned to Emily. "Miranda promised we could keep any money we make selling her stuff."

"I vote no," Emily retorted.

"Me too," Jake agreed.

"I vote yes," Jenny announced. "We need the money."

"That's two against two," Jake said. "We'll have to get Aunt Nan to break the tie."

"You know she'll vote yes," Sally pointed out. "She loves Miranda. So you might as well just let her be in the art show, without any more fuss. And you should come with us Sunday to make sand castings too," she added. "You'll get a great lunch. But that's not the point. The point is that we can ask real money for sand castings—a lot more than a quarter. They're different. They're worth something."

"What are they?" Jenny queried.

"Well, what you do is you dig out wet sand to make a mold—a face or something like that."

"But you have to do it backwards," Miranda explained. "If you want a nose that sticks out in the finished product, to make that you dig a hole for it in the sand. I mean, it's just the opposite of working with clay.

You can't shape sand into something that stands free."

Jake and Emily appeared utterly confused. But Jenny, who could visualize what Miranda was saying, nodded.

"And then," Miranda continued, "when you have the wet sand shaped the way you want it, you mix plaster of paris with seawater and pour it into the mold. It's dry enough to touch in half an hour. You pull the plaster of paris out of the sand, and you have sort of a mask."

"The back is just flat white plaster," Sally said, "but the front is beautiful. On the face, the plaster has picked up a thin layer of sand that sticks to it when it's dry. It makes your mask look like you carved it out of stone."

Jenny raised her eyebrows, a clear indication that she was interested. "You made these things, Sally?"

Sally nodded. "Two."

"I made two too," Miranda said.

"Miranda's are good. Mine are weird."

"But we could sell all four of them,"

Miranda assured her. "Some people like weird better than beautiful."

"And yours, of course, are beautiful," Jake said.

"Yes," Miranda replied.

"I should have known." Jake plopped down on a chaise and put his head in his hands.

"Yours'll come out weird too," Sally told Jake. "But you'll have fun messing around."

"You think I could make a castle?" he wondered.

Miranda nodded. "Maybe."

"Where are they?" Jenny said. "I want to see them."

"Oh, we didn't bring them home," Sally explained. "They're heavy. We couldn't carry them in our hands or in those little pouches on the backs of our bikes. We left them at Tanya's. Sunday we'll get someone to pick them all up with the car."

"Let's make them tomorrow," Jenny suggested. "We can have our sale on Sunday."

Miranda shook her head. "It's going to rain tomorrow."

"No, it isn't," Jenny said. "The TV said a nice weekend."

"Tanya says it's going to rain tomorrow. Tanya knows. She's a witch."

"Oh, Miranda," Sally sighed. "What did you have to go and say that for?"

"Well, it's true."

Emily turned to Sally. "You said it yourself, last night, to me."

"I didn't say Tanya is a witch," Sally snapped. "I said *she* says she's a witch." Sally regretted the words as soon as they were out of her mouth. Miranda's remark had made Miranda sound foolish. Sally's had made Tanya sound foolish.

"Well, what do you think?" Jake asked. "Is she?"

"She's awfully smart," Sally admitted. "That's all I know."

"And nice too," Miranda added.

"Also true," Sally agreed.

"I didn't think witches were nice," Jake said.

"They can be as nice or not nice as anyone else," Miranda explained. "You never know who'll turn out to be a witch. It's an inherited talent. She says maybe I have it. Actually, we're an awful lot alike."

"Then she must be nuts," Jake said.

"So what if she is," Jenny commented. "I want to learn how to make those sand castings. We'll all go over Sunday morning. We can have our art sale on Monday."

Sally woke the next morning to the sound of rain on the roof. "I can't believe it," her mother complained at breakfast. "Yesterday the weatherman promised us a nice weekend."

"You know Long Beach Island," Aunt Nan said. "It has its own weather. It's probably gorgeous today on the mainland."

Emily's nose was pressed against the big picture window overlooking the beach. "I don't mind rain once in a while," she said. "I like to watch it filling up the ocean."

Sally left the table and joined Emily in staring out at the sodden dunes. Emily turned and began to move away. Sally reached out, put a hand on Emily's shoulder and drew her back. "What's the matter with you, Emily?" she asked. "All last night you hardly spoke to me."

"I'm mad at you. What did you have to drag Miranda into our club for?"

"I didn't drag her into the club," Sally protested. "Only into the art show."

"She's a pain."

"Yeah, I know." Sally blew on the window. With her finger, she drew a transient face in the steam left by her breath. "But she thinks she has reasons."

"What reasons?"

"She made me promise not to tell."

Emily put her fist to her mouth as if she were speaking through a microphone. "Emily to Sally. Emily to Sally. This is me, your twin. Remember?"

"All right." Sally sighed with what she knew to be relief. "I'm sure Miranda didn't mean I couldn't tell *you*. Even she must know twins don't have secrets from each other. Only we can't tell Jenny or Jake. I promised."

"OK."

Sally took a deep breath. "Miranda thinks

we're mean to her because she's adopted."

"We're not mean to her."

"We're not exactly nice to her."

"She's a pain," Emily reiterated.

"Well, she doesn't know that. She thinks it's because she's adopted."

"Oh, for heaven's sake," Emily snorted. "Gloria's adopted. It's no big deal."

"Miranda thinks it's a big deal. She thinks it's why we don't like her."

"Boy, she's really sensitive, isn't she? Gloria isn't sensitive like that."

"We never talked to Gloria about it." Sally gazed at a pair of droplets racing each other down the window pane. "We play the Orphan Game, but what do we know about orphans, really? Maybe a lot of adopted people feel like that."

The rain lasted all day. Jenny and Jake arrived under an umbrella and spent the morning on the floor with Emily and Sally, playing cards. After lunch Miranda showed up, encased in a yellow slicker. "I wanted to come earlier," she said, "but my dad thought it was raining too hard. Finally he drove me over."

Jake threw down his cards. "I'm sick of this dumb game. Rain or no rain, I'm going out on the beach."

"Me too," Emily agreed. "There's no thunder or lightning. We won't get hurt."

"I can't go on the beach in the rain," Miranda said. "I promised my father. He said I might catch cold."

"Or melt," Jake said. "Wouldn't that be too bad."

"Are you coming, Sally?" Jenny asked.

Sally glanced at Miranda, looked away again, and nodded. "We won't be out long," she said.

"Don't count on it," Jake contradicted.

But Jake was wrong, and Sally was right. "Come on," Jenny shouted. "Run! The Denver Horror and Miss Priss are after us."

They chased each other onto the beach, waving their arms and screaming, pouring out all the energy that had accumulated inside of them during the long hours cooped up inside the house. In five minutes, their shorts and T-shirts were plastered to their skin, their hair dripped water into their faces, and they were chilled to the bone. "Hey, Julia, Octavia, see that shack," Emily screeched, pointing to her own house. "Let's take shelter there. We've got to, or we'll drown."

"I think Miss Priss is in there," Jake said, "but that's OK. I've found this magic crab that makes us invisible."

"We'll have to go to our house first and change," Jenny said. "Then we'll be over."

When Jenny and Jake returned, they were carrying a black plastic garbage bag filled with paper and crayons. "We're going to make flyers for the art sale," Jenny said. "We'll go around tomorrow on our bikes and put them in people's mailboxes."

Aunt Nan sat at the table with them to help. They needed a lot of flyers. "I hope it doesn't rain when we go to Atlantic City," Emily said.

"*If* we go to Atlantic City," Sally amended.

"Oh, Emily!" Jake groaned.

"Oh, Sally!" Jenny groaned at exactly the same moment.

Miranda laid down her crayon. "You're going to see *Carnival,* aren't you?"

Sally kept her eyes glued to the flyer she was lettering. "We might not go at all. We might not be able to raise the money. This art show won't bring in enough."

"I'd love to see *Carnival,*" Miranda said eagerly. "I'd love to see Atlantic City."

"Yeah," Sally replied. "I know. You told me."

For a long moment, absolute silence reigned at the table. Aunt Nan opened her mouth as if to speak, and then shut it again. It was Emily who said the words at last. "You can come with us, if we go."

"No, she can't!" Jake cried. "This is a Four Seasons trip. We'd have to raise another forty dollars if Miranda comes."

"One hundred and sixty, two hundred—what's the difference?" Sally shrugged. "They're equally impossible."

"You said that before," Jake returned. "But it isn't really true. Forty dollars means something."

"If Miranda's helping to raise the money,

she deserves to get some use out of it," Emily insisted. "That's only fair."

Miranda turned to Jenny. By now she knew their rules. "What do you say?"

"I'm against it," Jenny replied calmly.

Finally, Aunt Nan spoke. "So it's a tie, and I cast the deciding vote. Miranda comes."

"Then I'm *not* coming," Jake exclaimed. "Who wants to go with a bunch of girls anyway? Three is bad enough; four is impossible."

"Oh, Jake, don't be a jerk," Jenny scolded. "Of course you're coming. You wouldn't miss all that stuff on the boardwalk if you had to swim across the inlet to get there."

But later, after Cousin Lenny picked up Miranda, Jenny cornered the twins. "The Four Seasons is a *private* club, remember? What did you go tell Miranda our business for? Now look at the mess we're in. We've got to take her with us."

"It'll be all right," Sally said.

"She'll ruin the whole day," said Jake.

"We probably won't be going anyway," Sally pointed out.

"You're getting to be a real spoiler," Jenny accused. "Just like her."

"No, she isn't," Emily exclaimed hotly. "She's just telling the truth, that's all."

Jenny swept her art supplies into the black plastic bag and departed, taking Jake with her. Emily turned to Sally, her eyes liquid, her lips trembling. "I had to ask Miranda to come with us. The words just tumbled out of my mouth."

"They always do," Sally replied, her voice dark. "Like last December, when you invited the immediate world to Grandma's house for Hanukkah."

"It worked out OK."

"Yeah." Sally collapsed on the couch. "But I don't know if this will. Oh well, I don't blame you for asking her. I know why you did it. If you hadn't, I probably would have myself, sooner or later."

Emily plopped down next to her. "I wish Miranda hadn't told you she thinks we're mean to her because she's adopted. Now it's like we have to prove to her that she's wrong. Only Jenny and Jake don't know why we're suddenly sort of nice to her, so they get mad at us."

"And we can't tell them, because I promised not to." With her hands behind her head, Sally leaned back against the pillows. "I think," she said with a sigh, "I think Miranda is ruining our summer."

At quarter of ten the next morning, they set out on their bikes, Sally and Jenny leading the way, with Emily and Jake right behind them. Miranda pedaled hard, but still she couldn't quite keep up. A hot sun beat down on their backs. Already Sally could feel beads of sweat forming on her forehead. She could scarcely even remember the wind and rain of the previous day.

They turned left on Pearl Street. "It's three houses from the ocean," Sally called out, "on the north side of the street."

Jenny raced ahead, braking sharply at two-eighty-nine. Sally sailed up the driveway and dismounted. Seconds later, Emily and Jake arrived, followed shortly by Miranda. "Are you positive today's the day?" Jenny asked. "This place sure reads empty."

The five of them stared at the house. The yellow awnings were rolled up, the rocking chairs were bereft of their bright cushions, and the window shades were drawn down to the sills.

"It can't be empty," Sally said. She ran up the porch steps and pulled at the screen door. It was locked. She rang the bell. She knocked. She rang the bell again. No one answered.

Miranda, who'd run around to the back of the house, returned wearing a puzzled frown. "The back door's locked too. I tried it, and then I knocked and knocked. No one came."

Jake knelt down and tried to peer beneath the shade of one of the porch windows. "No good," he said. "I can't see a thing."

"I guess this Tanya really is a witch," Emily said. "She's disappeared like one."

"If she ever existed in the first place," Jenny remarked.

"She exists all right," Sally shot back.

"Come around to the side. I'll show you sand castings, like the ones we made, only they're Tanya's, so of course they're much better."

The five of them trooped around to the side porch. Geranium and philodendron plants no longer graced the wicker tables. The wall too was bare, a few rusty nails the only evidence that the sand castings had ever hung there.

"This place looks dead," Jenny said. "It looks as if no one's been here all summer."

Miranda sniffled and rubbed at one of her eyes. "I can't believe it," she said. "I can't believe Tanya would do this to me."

"I think you made her up," Jake said.

"Do you think Sally made her up too?" Miranda swallowed a sob.

"No one made her up," Sally retorted. "She exists. And so do the sand castings."

"Well, she sure isn't here now," Jenny said. "Maybe you misunderstood. Maybe she said *next* Sunday."

"She said today," Miranda insisted. "Didn't she, Sally?"

Sally nodded.

"I'm disappointed," Jenny said. "I wanted to learn how to do that sand casting stuff. And now all we'll have for our art sale are those dumb drawings. We'll be lucky if we clear five dollars."

"We could postpone the art show," Sally suggested. "Maybe Tanya will be back to-morrow."

"And what if she isn't? No, we better go ahead."

"Couldn't we wait just one more day?" Miranda begged.

"Maybe *you* could," Jenny said. "*I* can't."

Sally touched Jenny's arm. "Why not?"

"Because it's silly. It's silly to wait for someone who'll probably never show up." Jenny stomped off the porch, picked up her bike, and climbed on. Without waiting for Sally or anyone else, she pedaled away.

"She's really teed off," Sally said.

"Can you blame her?" Emily asked.

"No," Sally admitted. "I guess not."

Five

The twins' mother took one daughter along to help her each time she went to the laundromat. That afternoon it was Emily's turn. The other kids divided up to deliver flyers to the houses of all the people they knew on Long Beach Island. Sally ended up riding around with Miranda, a situation which didn't make her very happy. But that was how it had worked out, and there wasn't anything she could do about it.

"It'll be more fun if we all ride to-gether," Sally had suggested.

"We'll get done much faster if we take different areas," Jenny said. "I'll ride with Jake; you can ride with Miranda."

Miranda nodded. "Then Sally and I'll get back in time to make some pictures. We haven't done any yet."

"You better do a lot of them, Miranda," Jenny warned. "We're going to need a lot of them to make up for the sand castings we don't have."

"If you'd only wait a couple of days," Miranda suggested once again. "We could decorate shells, and I'd be able to do some more needlepoint."

"We don't have time," Jenny said. "We want to get to Atlantic City before our vacation's over."

"We've still got two weeks," Miranda said. "I know Tanya will come back. Something must have happened, but she'll show up, and then we can make the sand castings and have these really super things to sell. . . ."

"Listen, Miranda." Jenny faced her, her

hands on her hips. "I think it was stupid of you to get mixed up with a crazy lady."

"She is not crazy. There is absolutely nothing crazy about her."

"Oh, Miranda, come off it," Jenny said. "She calls herself a witch, and you say she isn't crazy?"

"Well, I think there can be witches," Jake announced judiciously. "And if there can be witches, then this lady might even be one of them. Her disappearing like that might even be proof."

Miranda eyed Jake with approval. "She told us it was going to rain yesterday. No one else knew that. Not even the guy on TV."

"She's an old lady," Jenny said. "Her arthritis bothered her. That's how she knew."

"She knows more than the weather. She knows lots of other things too."

Jenny glared at Miranda. "Like what?"

"Oh, lots of things."

"Forget about Tanya," Jenny snapped. "Just forget about her."

Jenny's words were like whips, stinging Sally as well as Miranda. "We're not going to forget about her," Sally almost shouted. "We like her."

"OK, so don't forget about her," Jenny retorted. "But don't talk to me about her. I'm sick of her." She turned to Jake. "Come on," she said. "Let's get started."

"Thanks, Jake," Miranda called.

"You're welcome, Miranda," Jake returned. "But just because your old lady friend might be a witch doesn't mean you're not a nerd."

Miranda didn't cry. She just stuck out her tongue at Jake, climbed on her bike, and pedaled away.

Sally did her duty. She helped Miranda shove flyers into the mailboxes of all the people they knew in the neighborhoods Jenny had assigned them. But her heart wasn't in it. She didn't care about the trip to Atlantic City anymore. The whole project had lost its appeal for her. Even though none of the other Four Seasons were with her, she could have played the Orphan Game inside her own head. But the Orphan Game had lost its appeal too. As a matter of fact, she felt as if the whole vacation had lost its appeal. It was turning out to be a terrible summer. In some way, that was Miranda's fault. Somehow, she'd gotten stuck with Miranda, and she saw no way of getting unstuck.

They pedaled up one wide, flat street and down another, each of them absorbed in her own thoughts. "Thank goodness," Sally sighed as she stuffed a flyer into the Hatfields' mailbox. "That's the last house. We can go home now."

"Let's leave one in Tanya's box," Miranda suggested. "Just in case she comes back."

Sally shrugged. "Oh, all right. We certainly don't have anything better to do." She didn't feel like sitting on the beach, ignored by Jenny and Jake. It was bad enough to be thrown into Miranda's company when they were alone together; it was a thousand times worse when they were with the others.

"We do have something to do," Miranda reminded her. "We have to draw. But it won't take us long to ride up to Tanya's. We'll still have plenty of time."

"I'm an awful drawer," Sally remarked glumly.

"You can't be worse than Jake. Emily's no genius either."

"Jenny was so down on a concert. That's because she can't sing. She thought an art show was a great idea. That's because she *can* draw. We have to do what Jenny's good at, not what anyone else is good at." Sally knew she was being disloyal to Jenny as she said those words. But hadn't Jenny been disloyal to her?

"It's too bad everyone can't just do what they're best at. Isn't it funny, Sally? I can sing like you can, and I can draw like Jenny can."

Miranda sounded so satisfied with herself it made Sally sick to her stomach. "Singing isn't my only thing," she replied coolly. "I'm a very good writer. I have whole notebooks full of stories and poems."

"With you, here? At the shore?"

"I brought one notebook with me." The

Orphan Game notebook. But Sally didn't say that. She never should have mentioned the Orphan Game to Miranda at all. If the others found out that she had, they'd probably drown her and Miranda both. Fortunately Miranda seemed to have forgotten all about it. Or if she remembered, she was keeping just as quiet about it as Sally had asked her to. Sally had to give Miranda credit for that.

"That's what you should do instead of drawing," Miranda said.

"What are you talking about?"

"Write some of the poems out in your very best handwriting, and then sell them."

"That's not such a bad idea." Actually, it was an excellent idea. Miranda might be an annoying person, but she certainly wasn't a dumb one. "Listen, Miranda," Sally said slowly, "can I tell you something?" She dragged her feet on the ground, skidding to a stop.

Miranda used her brakes. They stood side by side straddling their bikes in front of Tanya's house. "Go ahead, tell."

"Actually, I'm trying to do you a favor.

I mean, you told me how you feel about us, so I want to tell you how we feel about you."

"It's obvious."

"But you don't know why. You think you do, but you don't." Sally gave a brief moment's thought to the proper wording of what she had to say, and then decided there was nothing to do but plunge ahead. "Why do you brag so much? It just puts people off."

"Brag? I don't brag." Miranda didn't sound angry, only puzzled.

"You're always saying how good you are at this and how good you are at that."

"I wanted you guys to like me. I wanted you to take me in."

"That's no way to go about it. It doesn't work."

"Nothing would have worked," Miranda said. "I know that now."

"Not whining might work."

"I don't whine."

"Yes, you do. You don't hear yourself." Miranda frowned, and bit her lip. "Listen, every time you catch me whining, kind of look at me and raise your eyebrows."

"All right."

"But I don't think it'll make any difference." Miranda spoke with absolute conviction.

"Well, there's something else, Miranda."

"What?"

"Let's sit down."

They dropped their bikes on the lawn and climbed the stairs to Tanya's porch, where they rocked hard on the cushionless chairs, as if the movement made the conversation easier. "What if Tanya comes back and finds us?" Sally wondered.

"She won't mind."

"I guess not. Anyway, it sure doesn't *look* as if she'll be back."

But Miranda didn't want to talk about Tanya, at least not then. "What's the other thing, Sally?"

"You tell lies. Like that night you told your father you hadn't had any ice cream."

"So do you guys. Like the night Emily said you were going to bed, and you were

really going out." She stared at Sally un-flinchingly.

Score one for Miranda. Sally smiled a little. "Once we got to the Frosted Mug without you, and once you got there without us. So we're even."

"I guess everybody lies once in a while," Miranda replied.

"And usually gets found out, too," Sally said. "Lies are trouble. So is tattling."

"Who tattles?"

"You."

"I do not!" Miranda cried. "I certainly do not."

"You told on Jake. You told Aunt Nan he'd taken your needlepoint."

Miranda defended herself hotly. "I really did think he'd thrown it into the ocean. I really did. When I realized he hadn't, I was sorry I'd told. But you can't expect me to be perfect. Nobody's perfect."

Nobody's perfect. The phrase echoed in Sally's head. Nobody's perfect. Not Miranda. Not Emily, nor Jenny, nor Jake. And certainly not Sally. But imperfect Sally still had one or two more bones to pick with

Miranda. "You shouldn't have told just me you were mad at us, and then made me promise not to tell anyone else."

"Why not?"

"It's like you gave me a piano to carry around. I didn't ask to carry that piano."

"Well, just forget about it."

"I can't." Sally folded her hands in her lap and turned her head toward the street. "I told Emily."

Miranda's cheeks flushed bright pink. "I asked you not to and you did it anyway? That wasn't right."

"Emily's my twin. Twins don't have secrets. Everyone knows that."

"Well, I didn't. I don't know any other twins."

"You could have figured it out."

"You don't seem like twins."

"How do you know? You just said you're no expert. Like I'm no expert in orphans, you're no expert in twins." Sally forced her rocking chair to move faster and faster. "You don't tell a person a secret she's not supposed to tell anyone else without asking first if she wants to hear it. You weren't being fair."

"Did you . . . did you. . . ."

"Tell the others? No. I keep my promises."

"You do?"

Sally stretched out her foot, pressing it against the rocker of Miranda's chair so that all motion ceased. "Emily doesn't count. Can't you understand that? She's my twin. She's like part of me."

"I know why you told Emily. So you don't have to be the only one who feels sorry for me." Miranda wasn't whining; she was simply making a statement. "And here I was thinking you were nice to me just because you liked me."

"I do too like you." For the moment, Sally thought that was almost true. And as Miranda herself had said, everyone lies a little sometimes. "But I don't feel sorry for you." She released Miranda's rocker, and immediately it began to move again. "Maybe you're right, and I don't know anything about being adopted, but I still don't think the Orphan Game is sick, like you said. It isn't sick. It's normal. Lots of kids feel their mothers and fathers don't understand them. I bet just about all the kids in the United States have said to themselves at one time or another, 'These people I live with can't *really* be my parents. I must be adopted. My real father is the president, and my real mother is a movie star, and one day they're going to come to get me.' You don't have to really be adopted to think up things like that."

Miranda sat silently rocking, as if she were giving all that Sally had said time to sink into her brain. Sally jumped up, ran down to her bike, pulled a flyer from the basket, and shoved it into Tanya's mailbox. "I don't know why I'm doing this. Tanya isn't here," she called. "Come on, let's go home."

Moving slowly, as if her arms and legs were made out of lead, Miranda rose from the rocking chair and descended the steps. Sally didn't wait for her, but mounted her bike and sped away. *She'll catch up,* Sally thought. *She'll catch up soon enough.*

Back home, standing on the deck, she saw Jenny, Emily, and Jake lugging two inflatable rafts onto the beach. The lifeguards, who didn't permit rafting, left at five o'clock. The sight of her sister and cousins was a signal to Sally that it was nearly five now. Almost the whole day had been wasted.

Well, it wasn't going to be a total loss. Miranda could busy herself drawing pictures when she got back, if that's what she wanted to do. It was not what Sally wanted to do. She wanted to go rafting. She kicked off her sneakers and headed for the beach, pulling off the T-shirt covering her bathing suit as she ran.

She arrived as the lifeguards were climbing down from their stand. Jenny and Jake were seated on one of the rafts, and Sally joined Emily on the other. It was her raft too. Not one of them spoke, but they were busy nevertheless, staring at the lifeguards, willing them to leave.

One lifeguard was a guy and the other a girl. For two people who'd been together since ten o'clock in the morning, they seemed to have an incredible number of things to say to each other. But at last they pushed and dragged their stand up the beach, abandoned it near the snow fence, and departed.

As quick as seals slithering off rocks, Sally, Emily, Jenny, and Jake were up to their knees in the surf. They threw themselves side by side on their rafts, their feet kicking behind them, and paddled out beyond the breakers to watch the waves form.

"This one!" Emily shouted.

"No, no," Jake disagreed, "the next one is better."

They rode the wave Jake picked, screaming with delight as it carried them all the way in to the shore. Other kids were rafting too, including Chip, Amy, and Lisa. There was no sign of Miranda.

Later, their lips blue, their eyes pink and stinging, they left the ocean and carried the rafts back home on top of their heads. On her deck, Sally found Miranda seated at the table with white paper and crayons, drawing pictures of snow fences, sea gulls, and dunes. "These'll be enough," she said. "You don't have to do any."

"Good," Sally said. She remembered then to add, "Thank you."

Aunt Nan trotted up the stairs, arriving on the deck to peer critically at Sally over the top of her glasses. "You're shivering like a wet cat. Wrap yourself in one of those towels. They should be dry by now."

Sally lifted a beach towel from the railing and threw it around her shoulders, feeling the warmth of the sun-drenched terry cloth spread to the tips of her fingers and toes.

"What have you guys been doing all day?" Aunt Nan wondered.

"Delivering flyers for our art sale tomorrow," Miranda said. "You'll be there, won't you?"

"I wouldn't miss it for anything. I'm bringing some friends, too."

"Rich friends, I hope."

Nan shook her head. "I have no rich friends. But I do know someone on the island who's an artist. I should ask her. I hadn't thought of her until this minute."

"I know an artist," Miranda said.

"Too bad Denver's so far away," Aunt Nan said. "If it weren't, you could invite him—or her."

"She doesn't live in Denver," Miranda said. "She lives in Beach Haven."

"Oh?" Nan's eyebrows shot up in surprise. "What's her name?"

"Tanya."

"That's my friends's name!" Nan exclaimed. "Tanya Teretsky."

"I don't know my friend's last name," Miranda said.

"But it isn't very likely that there are two artists named Tanya living in a town as small as Beach Haven," Sally interjected. "Does your friend live at two-eighty-nine Pearl Street?"

"Well, she lives on Pearl Street," Aunt Nan said. "I don't remember the number. A house with yellow awnings."

"That's it! Your Tanya and our Tanya are the same person!" In her excitement, Miranda leaped to her feet, and then, as if she were a tire that had suddenly picked up a nail, she fell back into her seat. "I don't think she'll be at the art show."

"Actually maybe it's just as well," Sally said. "A lot of the art we're showing isn't very good."

"Let her be the judge of that," Nan said. "I'll call her up and invite her."

"She wasn't home this afternoon," Miranda said. "And she wasn't home this morning. She made a date to do sand castings with us, and when we got to her house she wasn't there."

"We were kind of mad," Sally said.

"I don't blame you," Aunt Nan agreed. "But you have to understand Tanya. Her mind is so busy with so many big ideas that sometimes she forgets little things like dates and appointments. I'll invite her right now." She stuck her finger into Sally's face. "As for you, young lady, take your shower and put on some clothes."

Sally obeyed. By the time she returned, Aunt Lou, Uncle Andy, Cousin Lenny, and Cousin Rhoda were inside the house with her parents, the Big Kids were throwing a football on the dunes, and the Little Kids were sitting on the deck with Aunt Nan.

"Did you reach her?" Sally asked. "Did you reach Tanya?"

Nan shook her head. "She wasn't there."

"I wonder where she went," Miranda said.

"It doesn't matter," Jenny interjected.

"Maybe she's with Antonio," Aunt Nan suggested.

"Antonio? She has some paintings by a guy named Antonio," Sally remembered.

"Her boyfriend."

"Her boyfriend!" Jake exclaimed. "That old lady has a boyfriend?"

"You don't even know her. What makes you think she's an old lady?" Nan queried sharply.

"Sally said she's an old lady." Jenny defended Jake.

"She looks like quite an old lady," Sally explained. "She's older than you, I bet." When Tanya had spoken of her boyfriends, Sally had supposed she'd been joking, or else talking about men she'd known centuries and centuries ago.

"So that," Aunt Nan returned drily,

"means she's tottering on the edge of the grave. And just a few days ago you were telling me I was more fun than the grownups."

"Well, you don't have a boyfriend," Jake said.

"How do you know?" Nan retorted. "Do you?"

Nan laughed and shrugged her shoulders. "I'll never tell."

"Where does Antonio live?" Miranda asked.

"In New York City. But he has a house on the island someplace too—Harvey Cedars, or maybe Holgate."

"Well, which is it?" Sally asked. The two towns lay in entirely opposite directions.

"H—H—that's all I can remember," Aunt Nan said.

"What's his last name? Do you think you could call him?" Miranda wondered.

"Oh drop it, already," Jenny said. "We don't have time to do the sand castings before the art show anyway."

"I just want to know why she wasn't there when she'd made an appointment with us. I didn't expect that. I didn't expect that at all." Miranda sounded as if she were about to cry.

"His name is Antonio Muir," Nan said. "You can ask Information."

Miranda nodded and hurried into the house. "She sure is hung up on this Tanya dame," Jake said.

"I can understand it," Nan replied. "She's a remarkable woman. If you met her, you'd agree."

A moment later, Miranda returned, unsmiling. "Unlisted number," she explained. "I said it was an emergency, but the operator said it doesn't matter if your mother's dying, they won't give out an unlisted number."

Aunt Nan reached out and took Miranda's hand. "Forget about it, honey. Let's go over to Bay Village after supper. We can walk around, maybe go on some rides. It'll be my treat."

Miranda wasn't listening. "I could find Antonio Muir, the way Dad found the Dietelbachs in Colorado Springs when Mom left the directions and their unlisted phone number on the kitchen table at home. He drove to the police station and asked the cops. They know where everyone lives in a town."

Raising her voice, Aunt Nan addressed them all. "You guys want to go to Bay Village tonight?"

"You'll drive us over?" Emily asked.

Aun Nan nodded.

"Great!" Emily said.

"Good," Jake agreed.

Together, Jenny and Sally said, "Sure."

Miranda said nothing. But except for Sally, no one noticed.

After dinner was eaten and the dishes done, Jake tugged at Aunt Nan's arm. "Ready now?" he asked.

She glanced around the crowded room, pointing at each girl as she called her name. "Sally. Emily. Jenny. Miranda. . . . where's Miranda?"

"Maybe in the john," Sally suggested. She walked down the hall and rapped on the locked bathroom door.

"Hold your horses," her father responded with barely controlled annoyance. "I'll be out in a minute."

Glancing into the bedrooms, and even peeking into the utility closet where she and Emily had hidden when they were toddlers, Sally saw no one. "Miranda's nowhere in this house," she reported upon her return to the front room.

"Maybe she's out on the dunes, playing football with the Big Kids," Aunt Nan said. The game had resumed as soon as dinner was over.

"Oh, Nanny, I don't think so," Sally said. However, she followed the others out on the deck and leaned over the rail. Lenny and Rhoda came too. Five kids were running and shouting in the sand, but the two extras were Dave and Monty Schreiber.

"She must have changed her mind," Jake said. "She's sick of Bay Village, I guess. Let's just go without her."

"Yeah," Jenny agreed. "She probably went on home."

"If she wanted to go home, she'd have asked me for the key," Lenny said. "She didn't go home."

Sally ran down the stairs and quickly inspected the array of bikes parked beneath the house. "Her bike's gone," she called out. "Miranda's bike is gone."

Lenny turned to Rhoda. "Did she say anything to you about going home?"

"She didn't say anything to me about anything," Rhoda replied coolly.

"Where could she be?" Lenny clenched his fists, unclenched them, and clenched them again.

Rhoda shook her head.

"How could you let this happen?" Lenny sounded frantic. "How could you let her just disappear like this?"

"How could *you?*"

"She could drown."

"Oh, Lenny," Rhoda sighed, "she's a super swimmer."

"The ocean is different. World-class swimmers can drown in the ocean." Lenny turned to the kids. "Didn't someone see her go?"

"She must have slipped out while we were cleaning up," Jenny suggested.

"Come on, Rhoda." Lenny grabbed his

wife's arm. "We'll get in the car and look for her, before it gets dark. I'll go in and tell them we're leaving."

"I have to get my purse," Rhoda said. Aunt Nan followed Lenny and Rhoda into the house, leaving the Four Seasons alone on the deck.

"Maybe she just wanted to go for a walk on the beach," Jenny said. "I mean, what's so terrible about that? I think Lenny's a little crazy when it comes to Miranda."

Sally sat down. She leaned over and stared at the floorboards, her head in her hands. She had a pretty good idea of where Miranda had gone. Maybe she ought to say something, and save Cousin Lenny from a nervous breakdown.

When Rhoda and Lenny came back out on the deck, Aunt Nan, Aunt Lou, and Uncle Andy were with them. "We'll go north in our car," Uncle Andy said, "and you can go south in yours. That way we can cover much more of the island before it's totally dark. Don't forget to stop back at your place first. I know she couldn't get in, but maybe she's sitting on the porch or something."

Sally stood up. "I think I know where Miranda went."

"You do? My God, why didn't you tell us?" Lenny shook his fist as if he were going to hit her.

"Calm down, Lenny." Rhoda placed a restraining hand on his arm.

"I just thought of it," Sally explained. "I think she went to find Antonio Muir's house."

"Who's he?" Lenny wanted to know.

Between Sally and Aunt Nan, they explained.

Lenny listened, staring at them intently. "What did she think she was doing, picking up strangers on the beach?" he grumbled when they were done.

"Not a stranger. My friend," Nan said.

"But she didn't know that. My God, when will she realize she's got to be careful?" His face grim, he started toward the steps. "I'll go to the police station and find out this Muir fellow's address."

Sally followed him. "Cousin Lenny. . . ."

He turned. "Yes?"

"Don't go after her."

"What do you mean, don't go after her?"

"She'll be all right."

"How do you know?"

Sally gazed directly into his eyes. "I know."

"You're a little girl, Sally. There are lots of things you don't know."

Why were grown-ups always so sure they were the only ones who understood anything? Wasn't it possible a kid might know more about another kid than the grown-ups did? "Miranda needs to find Tanya. Maybe you should let her do it. What bad thing will happen to her if you let her?"

"You want her to wander around alone at night?" Lenny cried. "She can't do that."

"Maybe she can," Rhoda said. "I agree with Sally. This isn't Hell's Kitchen. It's Long Beach Island. She'll be all right."

"Don't you care, Rhoda?" Lenny exclaimed. "Don't you care what happens to Miranda?"

"Of course I care. But putting her in a box isn't going to save her. You can't save your children. You can't. In the end, she won't thank you for trying so hard that you smothered her."

"We could sort of compromise," Sally suggested. "Emily and I'll go after her. We'll bring her back." *We'll do it right,* Sally thought. *We won't go marching into Antonio's house like the United States Marines.*

Cousin Lenny's mouth formed a tight line. He and Rhoda looked at each other for a long, silent moment. "Come back in an hour, either way," Rhoda said.

"If we don't hear from you, we'll call the police," Lenny added.

"Give them an hour, just an hour," Rhoda said. She took his hand, opened the screen door, and led him into the house. Aunt Nan, Aunt Lou, and Uncle Andy followed.

Jenny walked across the deck and stood next to Sally at the top of the steps. "Why is Lenny so nervous about Miranda?" she wondered. "He acts like she's going to die or something."

"He did have a little girl who died," Sally said. "Before Miranda. Remember?"

Jenny nodded. "But she was Rhoda's little girl too, and Rhoda doesn't act like that."

"People take things differently."

"You really think she's off chasing Tanya?"

Sally nodded.

"Why?"

"It's complicated."

"Try."

"Well, you know, Miranda kind of has this idea that Tanya is her real mother."

"That's nuts."

"She doesn't really believe it. It's more like she wishes it. But whatever's going on in her head, she has to straighten it out for herself."

Jenny nodded slowly. "Yeah," she said. "I guess Rhoda knows that. But Lenny doesn't."

"Maybe he'll learn," Sally suggested. "Sometimes people do change, I think. I hope."

Six

"Where are we going?" Emily had to shout to be heard above the noise of Bay Avenue traffic. Long Beach Island during the season was one place where there were more cars on the road at nine at night than there were at nine in the morning. Emily was pedaling along a few feet behind Sally, because the bike lane was too narrow for them to ride side by side.

"To the police station," Sally called over her shoulder.

"Why?"

"I'll explain when we get there. Hurry. We only have an hour." Sally, forcing her legs to move ever faster, lapsed into silence. She wasn't going to waste breath on explanations.

They rolled their bikes into the rack on the lawn in front of Beach Haven Borough Hall. The only lights on in the building shone from the rear, where the police station was located. "Why?" Emily asked again. "Why here?"

"Miranda gave us the clue herself," Sally said. "Don't you remember her telling us how her father found those people in Colorado Springs by asking the police? I'm sure here's where Miranda would begin looking for Antonio Muir, so here's where we're going to begin looking for Miranda."

"Boy, Sally, you've gotten very good at solving mysteries."

"Yeah," Sally returned with a sudden grin. "I watch 'Murder She Wrote' every Sunday night."

Emily put her hand on Sally's arm. "Do

you think the cops will tell us anything? We're only kids."

"I don't know," Sally returned. "But we have to try. There's no other way to start."

They hurried around to the side door lit by a bright electric sign on which the word POLICE was written in large red letters. Inside, a high counter stretched across the room, and behind it a cop sat pecking away at a typewriter. Voices of officers on patrol crackled through the radio, but his eyes never strayed from the keyboard.

Sally stood on tiptoe and leaned over the counter. "Pardon me, Officer," she called.

He turned, and as his gaze registered Sally's presence, he shook his head. "More little girls?" he said. "This is my night for the subteen set."

Sally shot Emily a significant glance.

The cop rose from his seat and came to the counter. "What can I do for you?"

"We're looking for Antonio Muir," Sally said.

The policeman scratched his ear. "So was she—the other one."

Stumped, Sally glanced at Emily once again. She didn't know what to say, because whatever she said had to match whatever Miranda had said, and of course she hadn't the faintest notion of what that was.

Fortunately, the cop was still talking. "What's going on at this Muir's place? An orgy for ten-year-olds?"

"Not an orgy," Emily offered. "A party. We lost the address."

"The other girl didn't say anything about a party. But she said she'd lost the address too. What's the matter with you kids, can't hold on to a simple address?"

"What did she look like?" Sally asked. "The other girl, I mean?"

"What's it to you?" the cop wanted to know.

"Maybe it was Miranda," Sally explained. "She's the one the party's for. Only she doesn't know it. It's a surprise. So she'd have given some other reason for wanting to find Antonio Muir's house. Of course, *he's* not giving the party—Mr. Muir, I mean. His son is."

"Alphonso Muir," Emily interjected. "He's the one who's ten. There's a whole bunch of Muir kids, you can't even count them. Alicia, Aspidistra, Aloysius, Augustus . . ."

"Don't forget Armageddon," Sally said.

"Or Ann. Or Art," Emily added.

"All adopted," Sally continued. "Like their mother and father. That's why all their names begin with *A.*"

"I hope *they* know where they live," the policeman said.

Emily smiled politely. "So what did Miranda say? What was her reason?"

"Yeah," Sally said. "We want to know what good excuse Alphonso thought up to get Miranda to his house. He's extremely creative." Emily poked Sally, far enough down so that the officer, still behind the counter, couldn't see.

"Well," he replied, "she said maybe her mother was there, and she had to find her mother. Someone was trying to reach her mother about an important business deal. Someone in California, where it's three hours earlier. I don't believe a word of it—

now. She was very convincing at the time."

"Because, don't you see, she was convinced." Sally shook her head. "That Alphonso, he's something. He probably made that call himself, just disguised his voice."

"Is her mother there?" the policeman wanted to know.

"Well, Miranda thinks she is," Emily said. "Why would she have said she was if she didn't think so?"

"You're asking me?" the cop cried. "I'm so confused I can hardly remember my own address. But Antonio Muir lives at fifty-two Beach Plum Road, in Holgate. I hope I don't get a call an hour from now to say he was robbed."

"By ten-year-olds?" Sally shot back, already half way out the door.

"A gang of ten-year-old girls," Emily added. "The newest thing in crooks."

"You forgot," Sally said. "Miranda's nearly eleven."

They were giggling hysterically as they pulled their bikes out of the rack and mounted up. They pedaled south on Bay Avenue at top speed, glancing back every other minute to see if a squad car was chasing them. Sally wondered if maybe you could go to jail for lying to the police.

But the police had better things to do than pursue youthful tellers of tall tales. Sally and Emily found their way to 52 Beach Plum Road without much difficulty. The large house of gray shingles faced the bay at the end of a long drive lined with tangled beach plum bushes. Though the place was new, its wide porches were trimmed with latticework and its peaked gables echoed the Victorian style of Tanya's house.

Light streamed onto the front porch through the screen door. Miranda stood with her back to the stairs, clutching the metal crossbar, her nose pressed against the screening. But when she heard Sally's and Emily's footsteps, she turned quickly, like an enemy spy surprised by the CIA. "What are you doing here?" she whispered.

"We came to find you," Emily whispered back.

"It was us or your dad," Sally said. Since whispering seemed to be the rule of the hour, she whispered too.

153

"Look," Miranda said. "Look through the screen."

The brightly lit kitchen seemed like a scene glimpsed at the movies. A man and a woman stood at the sink. While he scraped plates, she loaded them into the dishwasher. Their backs were to the girls so that not a word of their conversation was audible, but waving hands and bobbing heads revealed it to be a lively one.

Suddenly the man, his hands momentarily free, put his arms around the woman's waist. She turned her head. Sally could see that the woman was laughing. She could also see that it was Tanya. Actually she'd guessed that from the start, because of the orange hair, but now, seeing Tanya's face in profile, she was absolutely sure.

The man's lips brushed Tanya's ear. She put down the cup she was holding, and turned herself so that she was facing him and put her arms around his neck. Standing so that their bodies touched, they kissed.

Sally felt her face grow hot. "I guess that guy's Antonio," she said, still whispering.

"Look at that white mustache. He's sixty-five, if he's a day."

"It's disgusting," Miranda murmured. "Two old people, kissing like that, a big kiss, like on TV, not just a peck on the cheek."

She's right, Sally thought. People old enough to be grandparents were not supposed to act that way.

Sally returned her gaze to the screen door. Tanya and Antonio were standing as they'd been when the girls had first seen them, busy again with their cleaning up, as if the kiss were something that had never happened. "Listen, Miranda," Sally said. "We have to do something. We can't just stand here, staring."

Miranda pushed the doorbell.

"Who's there?" Antonio called as he crossed the kitchen.

"Miranda." Tanya must have heard her say that, because then she turned too.

"Who's Miranda?" Antonio asked as he unlatched the screen and opened it.

"I'm a friend of Tanya's."

"Well, come in, friend of Tanya's. Friends of Tanya's, I should say," he added as he caught sight of the other two. He smiled, and there were crinkles around his eyes. He sure looked like a grandfather—a very handsome one, but a grandfather nevertheless. If Sally hadn't seen what had been going on just a moment before with her own eyes, she never would have believed it.

Wiping her hands on a dish towel, Tanya came toward them. "How nice to see you, girls." She pointed to each one of them in turn. "Antonio, the one with eyes like the sea is Miranda. The dark pigtails belong to Sally, so that means the other one is Emily. Miranda, Sally, Emily, this is my friend Antonio."

They exchanged a polite series of how-do-you-do's. After that no one seemed to know what to say.

Tanya gazed at them thoughtfully. "Why don't we go sit on the back porch?" she said. "It overlooks the bay. Then you can tell us to what we owe the unexpected pleasure of this visit." She led the way through the kitchen and then the front room, a huge, entirely contemporary living-dining room combination with a vaulted ceiling into which skylights had been cut. The white plaster walls were hung with oil paintings, whose brilliant colors drew Miranda's eye like magnets. "You did these," she said to Antonio.

He nodded.

"I like them," she added, a defensiveness in her tone suggesting she'd just as soon not have had to say that.

But Antonio accepted the compliment as if it came without qualification. "Thank you," he said.

The porch jutted out over the bay, and sitting there, Sally could hear the gentle lapping of wavelets against the dock. "So peaceful now," Tanya said. "In the daytime there are traffic jams out here, the bay's so full of boats. They're fun to watch, but they make too much noise. I like it better now, when you can hear only the sounds the Indians who summered here hundreds of years ago must have heard."

Antonio began to talk about those Indians. He knew a lot about them. They'd lived by fishing off the surf and digging clams and crabbing—exactly the same activities that occupied most islanders to this day.

"How do you know that?" Miranda asked.

"They found a huge mound of shells at Tuckerton. In those days the mainland and the island were connected."

"If you'd like," Tanya said, "I can meet you at the Long Beach Island Museum tomorrow morning. You can see some of those Indian things. The museum is only open evenings, but I'm on the Board of Trustees, so they'll let me take you through."

"No," Miranda replied coolly. "We won't come."

"You're busy tomorrow? Then make it Tuesday."

"We won't come Tuesday either. We won't ever come."

"Why not?"

"Because you won't be there."

"Miranda! If I say I'll be there, I'll be there."

"That's not true." Miranda stared at her unblinkingly. "You were supposed to meet us this morning, for sand casting, at your house. We all got there, all my cousins and me. The only person who wasn't there was you!"

"Oh, my lord!" Tanya struck her head with the heel of her hand. "I have a brain like a sieve. I forgot. Miranda, forgive me, please." But she didn't seem terribly contrite. She and Antonio shared a glance and a secret smile.

"I'm afraid it's my fault," Antonio said. "I arrived unexpectedly and dragged Tanya away."

"He drove every reasonable thought out of my head." Tanya giggled like a little girl, which Sally found nearly as disgusting as the kiss. "He does that to me, you know."

"What happened to the sand castings?" Miranda asked. "The ones you had hanging on the porch? I wanted my cousins to see them. We wanted to make some for our art sale. We're trying to raise money for a trip to Atlantic City. The sand castings would have been good to sell, because they really look like something."

"I put them inside before I left," Tanya replied, "along with the cushions and the plants. Last year someone stole a couple of old wicker side tables from the porch—quite valuable, actually. It used to be that nothing like that ever happened in Beach Haven, but times have changed. I've learned to be more careful."

"I thought Antonio drove every reasonable thought out of your head." Sally knew Miranda's words were malicious, but she didn't blame Miranda for saying them.

Antonio laughed. "Tanya's work—that's different. She'd never forget to take care of one of her pieces, even if it was just a sand casting."

"*Just* a sand casting?" Miranda echoed. "They seem wonderful to me." Angry as she was at Tanya, she could not deny the power of her work.

"They break easily," Tanya said. "They're only plaster of paris with a coating of sand, not marble or bronze. Drop one and it's gone. And people are always dropping them, because they're quite heavy."

"We're going to get dropped," Sally said. "Dropped right into the ocean if we don't get home soon. We promised we'd be back in an hour."

Miranda stood up. "Good-bye, Antonio," she said quite formally. "Good-bye, Tanya."

"Have something to eat before you leave," Tanya offered. "Some ice cream."

"No thank you." Sally and Emily followed Miranda toward the porch door. The only way out was back through the house.

Tanya rose from her seat, the laughter gone from her face and her voice. "You're very angry with me, aren't you?"

Miranda didn't deny it. "You disappointed me."

"Because I forgot."

Miranda nodded.

"It's not just the forgetting. It's because something else—someone else—is more important to me than you are."

Miranda stared at Tanya in stony silence.

Sally was sure Miranda knew what Tanya said was true, but didn't want to admit it.

Tanya took both Miranda's hands in her own. "Miranda, I'm not your mother. I'm not your father. I'm just your friend. Did you ever make a mistake?"

"Yeah."

"So have I. And this morning I made another one."

"You're a witch. I thought witches didn't make mistakes."

"No. The last thing a witch is is perfect."

Perfect. There was that word again, perfect. Earlier, on Tanya's porch, Sally and Miranda had agreed they weren't perfect. Now here was Tanya herself, old and smart, admitting that after all these years, she wasn't perfect either. "Witches are only human, after all," she was saying. "You have to take me as I am—as I must take you. As everybody must take everybody, I suppose."

"To a certain extent," Miranda said. "Not if they're terrible. Not if they're really bad."

"As I certainly am not," Tanya returned.

"One thing about witches," Antonio interjected, "they're not very dependable."

Tanya responded in a voice full of injured surprise. "How can you say that, darling? I'm as dependable as the sun."

"As the moon, I'd say." Antonio was laughing at Tanya, and Tanya clearly knew it. "But you're right. We have to take each other as we are. If we don't, we'll end up with no one." He put his hand on Tanya's shoulder. "Maybe you ought to apologize to Miranda."

Tanya gazed directly into Miranda's eyes. "Miranda, I'm sorry. Forgive me."

Miranda whispered her reply. "I'll try."

"I'm not sure you really mean that," Tanya said, "but I'll act as if you do." She leaned down and kissed her on the cheek. "Now will you have some ice cream?"

"We can't," Sally said. "We really can't." She could picture Cousin Lenny pulling up to the front door at any moment now, like the sheriff in a cowboy movie, come to arrest the bank robbers.

"Listen," Antonio said. "I have a good idea. We can do the sand castings here, tomorrow. You and your cousins come in the morning. Tanya and I will give you the ones we make too, for your sale."

"But the sale is tomorrow afternoon," Emily pointed out. "We've passed out all the flyers."

"Get here by eight," Antonio said. "Sand castings don't take too long."

"What time is the sale?" Tanya asked. "And where?"

"On the Bergs' deck. Two P.M.," Miranda replied.

"I'll bring someone." Tanya turned to Antonio with a sly grin. "El Cheapo up at the Island Gallery in Loveladies has been bugging me for months for a piece."

"He's been bugging me too," Antonio said.

"He claims he can't afford my usual prices. He's worth a million at least, and I have no intention of making a charity out of him. But here's the skinflint's chance to get things with our names on them for a sum he's willing to pay."

"I've never before signed a sand casting."

He fixed soulful eyes on Miranda. "For you, dear, anything."

Miranda smiled. So did Sally. They couldn't help it.

"Including a ride home," Antonio added.

"We came on our bikes," Sally said. "But thanks anyway."

They got their ice cream, later. They sat eating it at the picnic table on the deck while Miranda explained about Antonio and Tanya to Jenny and Jake.

"Wow!" Jenny exclaimed. "Are they famous?"

"I don't know if they're famous," Miranda replied. "But this El Cheapo guy wants their work. He'll buy sand castings tomorrow. And so will everybody else."

"I guess Tanya won't forget the appointment this time," Jake said.

"She won't," Miranda replied with a nod. "Antonio's in on it. He's not a witch. He's dependable."

The screen door swung open and Lenny and Rhoda came outside. "We're going now, sweetheart," Lenny said to Miranda. "You've had a big day—and a big night. It's time you were in bed."

"I'll have to ride my bike home."

"Leave it here. You can get it to-morrow."

Miranda shook her head. "I'll need it first thing in the morning. By eight I have to be at Antonio's house."

"I don't think it's a good idea for you to ride that bike in the dark."

Miranda took a deep breath. Then words poured out of her mouth like a waterfall. "My bike has a light on the front and a reflector on the back. Bay Avenue has a well-marked bike lane, there's a street lamp on every corner, and the moon is out. The trip is less than a mile, and I'm eleven years old. Dad, *nothing* will happen to me."

Inside of her head, Sally was cheering. So, apparently, was Rhoda. "Nice speech," she said, smiling.

Miranda glanced at her mother, her eyes wide. Lenny opened his mouth, closed it again, and then reached out his hand to touch Miranda's cheek. "Don't be long," he said.

"Good night, all," Miranda called, as she started after him.

"Good night. Good night."

Sally heard Cousin Lenny's car pull out of the yard. A moment later, Miranda reappeared. "Just one more thing, Sally," she said. "Thanks."

Sally walked to the top of the steps. "Thanks for what?"

"For not letting him come after me."

"Oh. You're welcome."

Jenny stood next to Sally. "Hey, Miranda."

"Yes?"

"See you tomorrow."

Miranda smiled and waved. Then she was gone.

In the morning, early, Emily and Sally left the silent house. Their father had gone off even earlier, to play tennis. Their mother, Aunt Nan, and Lisa were still asleep. They didn't bother with breakfast, which was a good thing, because Tanya and Antonio had piles of sticky buns, orange juice, and milk waiting for them. Miranda, Jenny, Emily, and Jake worked with Tanya and Antonio in the sand under the back porch. Sally sat up above with her notebook and copied out her best poems on pieces of heavy creamy paper which Antonio had generously supplied. Fortunately, though she was a lousy drawer, she had lovely handwriting.

The notebook contained not only her own poems, but some favorites by other people as well. She copied out a couple of those too, and wrote their authors' names below.

At the Sea-side

When I was down beside the sea
A wooden spade they gave to me
    To dig the sandy shore.
My holes were empty like a cup;
In every hole the sea came up
    Till it could come no more.

—ROBERT LOUIS STEVENSON

It was a poem for very little children, of course. But Sally's mother never failed to recite it each year as they drove across the causeway onto the island, always with a kind of surprise in her voice, as if this was the first time she'd thought of it. Dad and the kids giggled, but they didn't stop her. That poem was the real beginning of the summer. It was part of the ritual of the beach, where everything important—the ocean and the sand and the people and the house—were reassuringly the same year after year. Now Sally knew the poem by heart too. If she and her mother both remembered it so well, she supposed it wasn't *just* for little children. It was for everybody. When she was grown up and had children of her own and came to the beach in the summer, even if it was a different beach, very far away from here, on the other side of the country, or even in Europe or Africa someplace, still she would recite it for them.

"Hey, Sally!"

Startled out of her reverie, Sally looked up. Jake was clinging to the porch rail like a monkey. "Come on down," he said. "Look at our stuff."

Sally carried her work into the house so it wouldn't blow away in the stiff island breeze and then went out through the kitchen. Under the house, which like all the houses along the ocean or the bay was built on pilings, twelve sand castings stood drying. Each person had made two and signed them with a stick in the damp plaster on the back. Sally walked from one to the other, admiring them. She thought it was probably a good thing she hadn't done any. Those who had needed a disinterested, admiring audience.

She would have known who'd made each one even without looking at the names. Jake had managed to construct towers, clumsy but nevertheless recognizable. Emily had created cats in relief, the second a marked improvement over the first. Emily learned quickly. Tanya, Jenny, and Miranda had cast masklike faces. Jenny's, like Tanya's, were men with elaborate curly beards and lots of hair on their heads, Greek gods perhaps. Miranda's faces seemed much smaller, gentler, softer. Maybe they were women, though it was hard to tell. Antonio had created two abstractions, circular whorls raised, like Emily's cats, in relief against a flat background. "They remind me of giant snail shells," Sally said.

"Maybe that's what they are," Antonio remarked.

Emily regarded them through narrowed eyes. "They look more like short Slinkies to me."

"Maybe that's what they are." Antonio agreed with her too.

"But they don't have to be anything except themselves," Tanya said, "anything except just what they are."

When the castings were dry, Antonio carted them all back to the Bergs' house in his pickup truck, and the kids arranged them on the deck. Antonio and Tanya didn't stay, but Aunt Nan helped with the setting up. The drawings and poems they laid out on furniture and counters in the living room. Three completed pieces of needlework, contributed by Miranda, were tacked to the wall.

It was a perfect day for an art sale—not raining, but overcast and a bit cool, so that people would be looking for things to do other than sitting on the beach. Almost everyone they'd invited came over. Emily and Jenny sat on stools at a small folding table and collected the money. Sally and Aunt Nan softened up prospective customers with cookies and lemonade. That had been Nan's idea. Miranda and Jake were the guides. No one had questions about the drawings, but everyone wanted to know all about the sand castings. Most people had never seen anything like them before.

The drawings and Sally's poems cost a quarter, with needlepoint and sand castings by kids priced at five dollars. Tanya's and Antonio's castings were marked at twenty-five dollars each, in accordance with Tanya's departing instructions. Everyone admired them, but no one bought them.

"If Antonio and Tanya are famous, none of our parents' friends know it," Jake griped. "We should have marked them cheaper. At least then they would have sold."

By quarter of four, with closing time only fifteen minutes away, everyone except the family had left. Emily was counting the money. "Fifty-six dollars and seventy-five cents," she announced.

"That's terrific!" Aunt Nan exclaimed.

"But not enough," Jenny pointed out. "Nothing like enough. We're going to have to do something else. We're running out of time."

"Maybe we'll just have to save up all winter and go next year," Emily suggested.

"We might not come back here next summer," Miranda said. "It's far for us. I want to go this year. I really do."

"Who doesn't?" Jake snapped. "But we have to be . . ."

He was interrupted by Tanya's voice calling up from the yard. "Are we too late? Is anything left?" Sally leaned over the rail and saw Antonio's red truck parked next to the steps. Tanya hurried up the stairs, followed first by Antonio, and then by a small man with a large belly who was dressed in rolled-up jeans, a tight striped sleeveless shirt, a beret, and about seventeen gold chains.

"Who do you think he is?" Jenny whispered, awed. "One more chain and he'd sink."

Antonio introduced the children to Aubrey Crispin. "El Cheapo?" Miranda mouthed to Tanya behind Mr. Crispin's back. Tanya nodded.

"What enterprisin' kiddies," El Cheapo drawled. "Are you thinkin' of goin' into competition with me?"

"Jus' for today," Jake drawled back.

"We were about to close," Jenny said. "But of course, for a friend of Tanya's, we'll extend our hours."

"I do hope there's something left for us," Tanya said. "If there isn't, Crispin will be so disappointed."

"Oh, a few odds and ends," Miranda replied casually. "Here, I'll show you." The girls led Tanya and Crispin around to the front of the deck, where the four sand castings remained, while Antonio went inside with Jake to inspect the drawings.

"You see the signature," Miranda said. She pulled one of the castings away from the wall so El Cheapo could note the name "Tanya Teretsky" cut into the plaster.

"Of course, anyone can scribble names," he said. "Even kids."

"Look at these castings," Miranda returned coolly. "Just look at them. Do they look like kids' work?"

He examined them carefully for a long time. Tanya made polite conversation with the girls, but even while she was talking, Miranda never took her eyes off El Cheapo, as if she suspected he might steal the sand castings if she glanced away for a second. "How much do you want for these?" he said at last.

"Twenty-five dollars each," Emily said.

"That's too much," El Cheapo replied. "I'll give you fifteen for Antonio's and ten for Tanya's."

"What!" Tanya screamed. "Since when is a Muir worth more than a Teretsky?"

"Antonio isn't known as a sculptor," El Cheapo returned with a lift of his chin. "His are unique."

Sally wasn't listening to the argument. She and the other girls were standing at the rail, whispering. Finally she turned and faced El Cheapo. "Twenty-five dollars each, or nothing," she announced firmly. "This is not a flea market."

"Really, Crispin," Tanya scolded, "how can you stand here bargaining with children over pennies?"

"I see no difference between children and grown-ups when it comes to business," he replied primly. "They all take advantage of you, but children simply make use of different advantages—like their youth and charm and *apparent* innocence."

"Twenty-five dollars each," Miranda repeated.

"What a bargain you're getting, Crispin," Tanya said. "It's actually sinful."

Crispin reached into the pocket of his jeans, pulled out a money clip stuffed with bills, and carefully counted out three twenties and four tens. Emily grabbed them from his fingers before he could change his mind. "You're tough little girls," he said. "I don't think it's a bit becomin'."

"Ignore him," Tanya said. "Come on, Crispin, let's go. As a reward for your overwhelming generosity, I will serve you some of my unbelievably delicious, world famous bouillabaisse for supper. Only a witch could create such a stew."

Jake opened the door and stepped out on the deck, followed by Antonio, carrying several drawings under his arm. "He bought one by each of us," Jake said as he pressed a ten-dollar bill into Emily's hand. "He said to keep the change."

"Let's see, fifty-six seventy-five from before," Emily figured as she arranged the bills and coins into neat piles, "and a hundred and ten now. That makes one hundred sixty-six seventy-five. We've got twelve seventy-two we all coughed up over the past week. So we're short just twenty dollars and fifty-three cents. We've got just about that much in the Four Seasons savings account. Someone will lend it to us, and we'll pay them back when we get home."

She looked up, a big grin stretching across her face. "We made it!" She began a chant, jumping up and down to the rhythm of her words. "We made it! We made it! We made it!" Jake put his hands on her shoulders, chanting and jumping too. Sally, Jenny, and Miranda fell into line.

"Me too!" Tanya shouted. She placed her hands on Miranda's shoulders and joined the jumping. Aunt Nan was the next to succumb. Antonio couldn't resist either, and a moment later, he too was chanting and jumping, jumping and chanting.

"You people are crazy," El Cheapo cried. A sand casting under each arm, he retreated down the stairs.

"We made it! We made it! We made it!" the leaping line shouted. "We made it! We made it! We made it!" They jiggled and joggled around and around the deck until, exhausted at last, they collapsed laughing into chaise lounges and chairs and even onto the floor.

Seven

The Four Seasons stood in the prow of the Black Whale, watching the towers of Atlantic City slowly growing larger and clearer. "I'm going to walk up and down the whole boardwalk," Jake said. "I'm going to look in every souvenir shop for that shell."

"What shell?" Sally asked.

"Don't you remember? You're the one who invented it. The one that got sold at the garage sale. The one that holds the secret to the orphans' identity. You said it had ended up in Atlantic City. That's why the orphans have to go there."

"Thanks, Marchmain. Thanks for reminding me." The ship's deck rocked gently, soothingly beneath Sally's feet. She narrowed her eyes as she gazed across the inlet. She'd never been to Atlantic City before, yet the skyline seemed strangely familiar. "I'm going to tell you something. We're going to find our way around Atlantic City just fine. It looks exactly like our home planet."

"Our home planet?" Emily exclaimed.

"I'm remembering, I'm remembering." Sally placed the back of her hand against her forehead. "It's coming back to me. We were born on another planet. Its name is . . . let me see . . . O . . . Osh . . . Osheanna!"

"Kids!" Aunt Nan's voice ended the Orphan Game—for the moment. With the others, Sally turned to see Nan and Miranda coming toward them across the deck carrying the sodas they'd gone inside to buy, Aunt Nan's treat. "Listen," Nan said as she handed the cans around, "we still haven't decided about the tickets."

"Let's figure that out when we get there," Jenny suggested.

"I don't want a raving fight going on in front of the theater," Aunt Nan insisted. "Or on the boardwalk, or in the restaurant. I'd die of embarrassment. We've got to make up our minds who's sitting where right now." From her pocketbook she extracted the tickets she'd picked up at the Bellevue two days before. The show was almost sold out, and she hadn't been able to purchase six seats together. Two were down front, the other four were way in the back.

"The fairest thing to do is to draw lots," Jenny said.

"I don't think that's fair at all," Miranda complained. "The two people who contributed the most to this trip should be the ones to sit up front."

"What do you mean, contributed the most?" Jake queried sharply.

"Raised the most money," Miranda said. "That's me. I raised the most. Except for Tanya and Antonio, of course. But of the kids, I raised the most. My stuff brought in the most money because there was the most of it."

"Listen, Miranda," Jake said, "you're not even a member of the Four Seasons. Twenty dollars came out of our treasury. You're getting the benefit of that, even though we're just letting you come with us out of the goodness of our hearts. So don't start thinking you can make up the rules."

"Yeah, sure, the goodness of your hearts." Aunt Nan waved the tickets under his nose. "Any more talk like that and I'll take one of these and throw it into the ocean. I'll know exactly which one, too. Yours!"

"Oh, Nanny," Miranda said, "don't pay any attention to him. He's just teasing me."

For a moment Jake appeared startled, but he made a rapid recovery. "That's right. I'm just teasing. I always tease Miranda."

"And if not Miranda, somebody else," Emily said.

"That's my way," Jake added with a shrug.

"Everyone knows that," said Jenny.

"Do they?" Aunt Nan asked. She was looking at Miranda.

"Yes," Miranda agreed, "everyone knows that."

Aunt Nan relaxed. "All right, then. So what do we do with the tickets?"

"We draw lots," Sally said. "We're all for one in this club, and one for all. We all do our best."

Once again, Aunt Nan directed her attention to Miranda.

"Draw lots," Miranda agreed.

"I'm not in the lottery. I'll definitely sit in the back." Aunt Nan tore five sheets of paper out of a notepad in her purse and marked two with an X. She folded them, shuffled them up in Jake's Mets cap, and passed it around so each of them could pick. Jake and Sally won.

The Black Whale slowed down and inched its way carefully into the pier. A crewman leaped from the deck onto the wooden dock, and another tossed him a rope which he tied to a bulkhead. Someone else dropped an anchor. A gangplank was lowered. Sally, Jenny, Jake, Emily, and Miranda rushed down it so quickly Aunt Nan had to yell to them to wait up.

They toured the entire length of the boardwalk. The twins' dad said all the money from gambling hadn't done a thing to improve it. He said it was just as tacky, just as honky-tonk as it had ever been, like a cheap fireman's carnival in a tiny country town. But Sally didn't care, and she knew none of the other kids did either. There was so much to do, so much to see. They played ski ball and keno. They ate cotton candy. They rode the merry-go-round, the Ferris wheel, and the bumper cars, but rejected the motorized open jitney filled with senior citizens as too expensive. They sat in an auction gallery and watched people go crazy bidding on television sets and gold necklaces they could have bought for half the price in any ordinary store. They inspected the shells in trays in souvenir shops as carefully as if they were diamonds.

"There are better shells on the beach for

free," Miranda said. "What do you want to waste money on these for?"

"I don't." Jake poked Sally in the ribs. "None of these are right. They're just ordinary."

Sally nodded. "The one we want is somewhere else," she whispered.

They put quarters down on a wheel of fortune, also a waste of money, except for Emily, who won a three-foot-high rabbit with long, straggly electric blue hair. "What are you going to do with it during the show?" Jake asked. "We can't afford to buy it a ticket."

"He'll sit on my lap," Emily said.

"Does he have a name?" Sally asked.

Emily grinned. "El Cheapo."

A child no more than two years old was sitting on a bench with her parents. When Emily strolled by carrying the rabbit, the little girl jumped down and ran toward her. She reached up and stroked the blue fur, which came off in clumps in her hand. "Nice bunny," she said. "Nice bunny."

The mother grabbed the little girl by the

arm. "Bad baby," she shouted. "Bad, bad baby. Don't touch!" And she slapped her hand.

The child started to cry. "It's all right," Emily said. "She can pet my bunny." But the mother shook her head and pulled the screaming child back to the bench.

"How mean," Emily said. "That was the meanest mother I ever saw."

"You'd think that wasn't her kid," Jake said. "You'd think she was adopted or something."

"I'm adopted," Miranda announced immediately. "My mother never pulled my arm out of its socket."

"You know," Jake said, "I forgot. I forgot you were adopted."

"Some adopted mothers are mean to their kids," Miranda said, "and some are nice. Just like birth mothers."

"Yours is nice," Jake said.

"She's OK."

They walked on, in silence for the first time that afternoon. Sally glanced at Miranda. Her forehead was wrinkled, and her lips were pressed together. Was she going to pout for hours because of one thoughtless crack? Was she going to cast a shadow on their whole wonderful day? Were they all right back where they'd started from?

But when she spoke, it was clear that Miranda had been thinking, not brooding. "You know, Jake, at first I thought that was why you guys were mean to me. Because I was adopted—not your real cousin."

"Maybe we didn't like you too much," Jake returned, "but we never thought you weren't our real cousin."

Miranda nodded. "Just now, you didn't even remember I was adopted."

Jake graciously clarified the situation. "We didn't like you because you were a pain in the neck."

"Jake!" Aunt Nan scolded.

"You didn't like me because you didn't like anybody," Miranda said. "You were a closed corporation."

"I knew what you thought, because you told Sally, and Sally told me," Emily said. "So now we all know how you felt. And you know how we felt. So now maybe we can forget it."

"Yeah," Sally agreed. The conversation was making her nervous, and she wanted it to be over. She glanced at her watch. "We'd better go for dinner. It's six o'clock, and the show's at eight."

"I'm starved," said Aunt Nan. "And tired. I can't believe you kids walked the *whole* boardwalk. No, I can believe that. What I can't believe is that I walked it with you." But she didn't look like a tired lady as she hurried forward holding Emily's and Miranda's hands.

"Listen, Octavia," Jake said, "if that shell isn't in a souvenir shop here in Atlantic City, where do you think it is?"

"I don't know," Jenny replied, without interest. Her eyes were fixed on the three figures up ahead. "Come on, guys," she urged. "Let's catch up to the others."

At the Seafood Garden, they gorged themselves on fried fish, hot muffins, coleslaw, and corn on the cob. Enchanted, they watched a gorgeous glittery carnival unfold before them on the stage of the Bellevue Theater. Afterward, on the Black Whale, they licked ice cream cones and clustered around the accordion player, begging him to play the *Carnival* theme, "Love Makes the World Go 'Round," again and again and again. Sally never thought about Marchmain, Julia, Juliette, or Octavia, not even once.

The twins pulled their suitcases from under their bed. They had to start packing. Five days had passed since the trip to Atlantic City. The next morning, early, they were going home.

"There was a time," Sally said, "when I thought this might turn out to be the worst summer of my life. But actually it was the best."

"What was the best day of the best summer?" Emily asked.

"Atlantic City, of course," Sally said.

"Atlantic City, of course," Emily agreed. "And what was the best thing on the best day?"

"The show," Sally said. "We ought to do *Carnival* at school. I'll play Lili. Maybe Jake could be the puppeteer."

"You want to marry Jake? Ugh."

"It'd just be a show, Emily, just pretend, like the Orphan Game."

Emily picked up her electric blue rabbit. He'd lost so much hair in five days that he looked as if he had some weird skin disease. But that didn't seem to diminish Emily's affection for him. "For me, the best thing was winning El Cheapo." She tried to shove him into the suitcase, but he wouldn't fit. "I'll have to carry him home on my lap, the way I sat with him in the theater," she said as she propped him up against her pillow. "I knew from the moment we got in the car for the trip down that this was going to be a great summer. Why did you ever think it was going to be terrible?"

"Because of Miranda," Sally replied.

"Miranda isn't so bad."

"That's what you think now. It isn't what you thought in the beginning. I felt like a rubber band. She was pulling me on one side, the rest of you were pulling me on the other. Then I told you, and it was better. And now Jake and Jenny have decided she's OK too, but really, she hasn't changed. Not much, anyway."

"I guess we've just gotten used to her."

"We've gotten to know her. We don't just see the bad parts. We see the good parts too. And the same with her and us." From the bureau drawer, Sally pulled out four pairs of socks she'd never once had on her feet the whole time she'd been at the beach and threw them into her suitcase. "Boy," she sighed. "I'm wishing all year could be summer."

The bedroom door swung open to reveal Jenny carrying a plastic bag from which a long, rolled-up scroll stuck out. "Hey, you guys," she announced, "special meeting of the Four Seasons."

"We have to pack," Sally replied.

"It's too early to pack," Jenny said. "Wait until it's dark. Once you start to pack, you really know you're leaving. That's why in our house we never do it until the last minute."

"I'm coming," Emily said, grabbing her rabbit. "So is El Cheapo."

When all of them, including Aunt Nan, were settled on the deck, Jenny placed the plastic bag in front of her and banged her fist on the table. "I called this meeting," she informed them in her loud, slow president's voice, "to take up a special issue." She paused portentously and looked around the table. "I want to propose a new member."

"A new member?" Emily said. "We can't have a new member. There can't be five seasons."

"An honorary member," Jenny amended. "This is someone who lives too far away to be a regular member anyway."

"Oh," Jake said. "You mean Miranda."

Jenny nodded. "Any objections?"

Jake didn't say a word. Neither did anyone else. Jenny opened the plastic bag and pulled out the scroll, which was tied with a red ribbon. "I made this," she said, "so

Miranda can take it home and hang it in her room. It'll be a kind of souvenir of the summer."

"Weren't you taking a chance?" Jake queried. "Suppose we *had* objected?"

"I knew you wouldn't."

Sally unrolled the certificate and examined the large black letters Jenny had inked on the white paper in her best calligraphy. "This is really beautiful."

"Thanks," Jenny replied.

"Let's take it to her," Sally suggested.

"I'll drive you," Aunt Nan offered.

Inside Miranda's cottage, the front room looked exactly like the one they'd just left, littered with cardboard boxes and canvas duffel bags. Cousin Rhoda stood in the middle of the mess, holding a giant can of baked beans in her hands. "Is this worth lugging two thousand miles across deserts and mountains?" she asked as they trooped into the house.

"No," Aunt Nan replied.

"Then take it off my hands, please," Rhoda begged.

"I never eat baked beans," Aunt Nan responded. "They give me gas."

"But we eat them, with hot dogs," Sally said. "You can serve them to us at the next Four Seasons meeting."

Rhoda held out the can. "I guess I am now the proud possessor of the one thing I've always longed for," Aunt Nan sighed as she took it. "The world's largest can of baked beans."

Miranda, wearing a terry-cloth cover-up over her dripping bathing suit, appeared at the door. "I saw you guys from the beach. What are you doing here? You never come here."

"We're making a presentation," Jenny said. "You'd better come in and sit down."

Jake pushed a box from a chair onto the floor. "Here, Miranda, on this."

Miranda obeyed. The other four stood around her in a semicircle, in the middle of which Jenny unrolled the scroll. With a flourish, she handed it to Miranda, who took it. Silently, slowly, she read it over to herself. Then, as if she wanted to make sure she'd gotten it right, she read it again, out loud.

Be it known that
MIRANDA SLAVIN
has been elected an honorary member of
THE FOUR SEASONS
with all the rights and privileges
thereto pertaining.
August 28, 1987
Jennifer Alexander, president
Jacob Alexander, vice president
Emily Berg, secretary-treasurer
Sally Berg, member
Anne G. Schiff, adviser

Miranda lowered the scroll to her lap. "I can't come to meetings," she said.

"That's all right," Emily replied. "I'll send you copies of the minutes."

Miranda turned to her mother. "Do you think we'll come back to Long Beach Island next summer?"

"I don't know, darling. It's too soon to talk about next summer. So many things can happen in a year."

"I've got something for you," Miranda said. She ran into her room, returning a moment later with the snail shell in her hand. She dropped it on the table in front of Jenny.

Jenny picked it up and examined it closely. "This is a perfect snail shell. It's the best one I've ever seen."

"I found it. I want you to have it, all four of you."

"Aunt Nan can keep it in her curio cabinet," Emily said. "Then when we have our dinners, she can put it in the middle of the table so we can all see it."

"And think of you," Sally said.

"Thank you, Miranda," Jake added.

For a moment Sally thought she might cry. But then Jenny jumped up. "Come on, guys," she cried. "We've never been on Miranda's beach. Let's try it."

Miranda glanced at her mother. "Go ahead, honey," she said. "Nan'll help me."

"No more cans," Nan said. "I'm not planning to open a grocery store."

They left their flip-flops in a row by the

snow fence. "Hey, Miranda," Jake said, "when's your birthday?"

"February twenty-sixth. Why?"

"Good. That's winter. We didn't have a winter until now. Your name is Febrita."

"What kind of name is that?"

"It's your orphan name," Jake said. "I'm Marchmain, Sally is Julia, Emily is Juliette, and Jenny is Octavia. We're trying to escape from Matron. She runs the orphanage. We're trying to find out who our parents are—or were. We're trying to find out why they left us in such an awful place. You can catch up on all of it by reading the Record in Sally's notebook."

"This game is a secret," Emily said. "No one knows about it but us, not even Aunt Nan."

But Miranda did know about the game. She knew because Sally had told her. "Maybe Miranda doesn't want to play," Sally said.

Miranda didn't hesitate. "Of course I want to play. But I don't like my name. It's too hard to say. Couldn't I just be Rita?"

"Run, Rita," Jake shouted. "Run! Matron is after you."

Miranda shrieked, ran over the dune, and jumped the snow fence. The others followed, screaming at the top of their lungs. They hurtled into the warm, foaming surf and swam out beyond the breakers. Later, when Aunt Nan stepped out onto the deck, she could see them, three light heads and two dark ones, bobbing joyously in a tight little circle between the clear green sea and the cloudless, sun-glazed sky.

Barbara Cohen

is the author of many books for young
people, including picture book texts, re-
tellings of biblical stories, and novels. Her
first book, *The Carp in the Bathtub,* is con-
sidered a modern classic. *Molly's Pilgrim,* a
Thanksgiving story, was made into a film
which won an Academy Award in 1986.
Ms. Cohen has received National Jewish
Book Awards and the Association of Jew-
ish Libraries Sydney Taylor Body-of-Work
Award. Several of her works have been
named Notable Books and Best Books for
Young Adults by the American Library
Association. Her most recent novel, *The
Christmas Revolution,* also features the twins
Emily and Sally Berg and their cousins
Jenny and Jake. Ms. Cohen lives in Bridge-
water, New Jersey, and spends summers
on Long Beach Island, the setting for *The
Orphan Game.*